Dear Reader,

I've always loved old movies from the thirties and forties. Who could ever forget Gable and Colbert sharing that motel room in *It Happened One Night*, or conniving reporter Jean Arthur out to "get" Gary Cooper in *Mr. Deeds Goes to Town*, or unworldly paleontologist Cary Grant getting mixed up with spoiled heiress Katharine Hepburn and her pet leopard in a screwball search for a missing dinosaur intercostal clavicle bone in *Bringing Up Baby*?

Like Grant's character, Donovan Kincaid is the quintessential absentminded professor. As a scientist, he deals in unemotional, observable data. He believes facts are facts, fantasies are fate. Until his college sweetheart Brooke Stirling makes a sudden, unexpected reappearance in his life. And suddenly this man of unwavering logic finds himself emotionally torn between two females—the woman he once loved, then lost, and a television-addicted gorilla named Gloria he can't afford to lose.

Donovan and Brooke's romance was first featured in Harlequin Temptation. I had a lot of fun writing their story and I hope you have as much fun reading it.

Warmly,

JoAnn Ross

JoAnn Ross

Tempting Fate

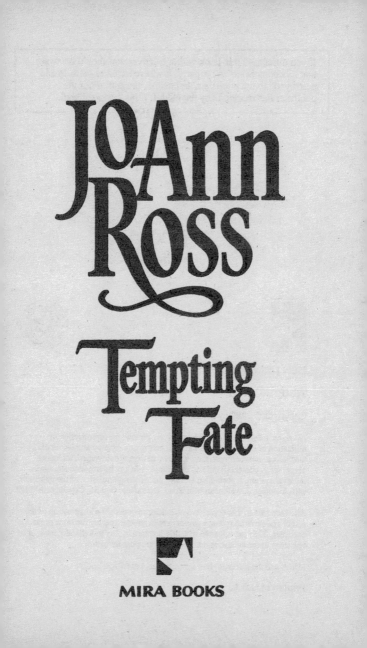

MIRA BOOKS

ISBN 1-55166-157-8

TEMPTING FATE

Copyright © 1987 by JoAnn Ross.

Chapter One

Donovan Kincaid did not believe in fate. Nor did he indulge himself with fanciful notions concerning coincidence, luck, or the ridiculous conjecture that the position of the stars could dictate one's future. As a scientist, he dealt in facts. Unemotional, observable data.

Even when confronted by the existence of seemingly unfathomable phenomena, Donovan believed that if given sufficient study everything could ultimately be explained. If he had been the type of man to waste time dissecting emotions, he would have realized that he had always found those inalterable truths vaguely comforting. As it was, he had never given the matter a great deal of thought. Facts were facts, fantasies were fantasies. And never the twain should meet.

As he jogged across the wet green grass of Marston Quadrangle, Donovan sought to come up with a logical reason for why he was finding the upcoming meeting so distracting. As the newly hired Director of Appropriations, Brooke Stirling held the key to his future in her hands. Yet as disturbing as he found that prospect, Donovan was also bothered by the idea that there was no rational explanation for her unexpected reappearance in his life. Just as there was no comprehensible justification for why he was feeling both anticipation and apprehension at the same time.

Deep in thought, he failed to notice the coed who stopped to watch as he ran by, her gray eyes filled with feminine appreciation. If asked to give a description of himself, Donovan would have rattled off a list of dry statistics that, while proving accurate enough, would not have revealed the essence of the man.

His height and weight—six foot three, one hundred seventy pounds—suggested a tall, lanky build. A youngish Jimmy Stewart type, perhaps. But women's eyes were invariably drawn to the play of smooth, taut muscles under his shirt, lean hips and strong, subtly muscled legs. Just as he would fail to describe his rangy, athletic build, Donovan would never offer the embellishment that his chestnut hair was tipped with gold. Nor would he think to compare his intelligent green eyes to newly mined emeralds. Such observations, viewed through the eyes of the beholder, would have been subjective and Donovan Kincaid dealt solely in objective, verifiable facts.

A quick, hopeful glance at the leather-banded watch on his wrist only corroborated what Donovan already knew. He was late. *Terrific way to make an impression, Kincaid,* he castigated himself irritably. In a futile effort to make up time, he picked up his pace. Reaching the Carnegie Building, he took the stone steps two at a time. As he ran down the tiled hallway, Donovan belatedly remembered he wasn't wearing a tie. Cursing softly, he yanked a rumpled bit of knit fabric from his jacket pocket and looped it hurriedly around his neck, managing something that remotely resembled a half Windsor knot just as he reached the office door.

Donovan promptly found that his way to Brooke Stirling's inner office was barred by a stocky woman whose gray hair brought to mind a Brillo pad and whose steely eyes behind dark horn-rimmed glasses were filled with overt censure.

"We've been waiting for you, Professor Kincaid," the guardian of the door huffed.

Her high-handed manner took Donovan back to when he was ten years old and had been summoned to the principal's office for setting fire to his classroom. Despite the fact that the youthful act of arson had been unintentional—an experiment for the science fair had gone awry—the principal's expression exactly mirrored the vexed one currently worn by Brooke's thickset receptionist.

"I was working in the lab," he apologized, "and time just slipped away. You know how it is." He gave her his most winning smile.

When he chose, Donovan could be charming. Too often, his requests for research money had depended on that ability. As an added bonus, it had not escaped Donovan's notice that the slightly crooked, boyish grin worked wonders with females of all ages.

Unfortunately, in this case, it fell decidedly flat. Ignoring him completely, the scowling woman punched the button of the intercom and announced his presence.

As Donovan was finally granted entrance to the inner sanctum, a slender, dark-haired woman rose from behind a gleaming expanse of desk.

"You're getting better," Brooke Stirling greeted him easily. "I can remember a time when if you only kept me waiting three hours, I considered it a good day."

"I must have been a callous bastard in those days."

"There were times." As she held out her hand, Brooke's accompanying smile was genuine. "It's good to see you again, Donovan."

How could he have forgotten that lush voice? During their college days, the deep, smoky tones had not meshed with Brooke Stirling's coltish, all-American good looks. Now, twelve years later, she had definitely grown into it.

His eyes swept over her in an appraising gaze. "You're looking well, Brooke."

That was an understatement. During the intervening years, Brooke had metamorphosed into one of the most sophisticated women Donovan had ever seen. Intellectually he knew it would have been folly to expect the young woman who had practically lived in a faded Beethoven sweatshirt. After all, it was against those inviolate laws of nature for anyone to remain college age forever.

She reminded him of someone. Donovan searched his memory and came to the unwelcome realization that Brooke bore a striking resemblance to her mother. He could only hope that she had not also become as hard and unbending as Carolyn Stirling. He searched her eyes—bright golden eyes that slanted upward slightly at the corners—for a clue and found nothing.

"You're looking well, too," Brooke answered after a moment.

Why had she thought it would be so easy? Despite the years, despite what had happened between them, it could have been yesterday that she and Donovan had last been lovers.

As her tawny eyes submitted him to a slow appraisal, Brooke marveled at Donovan's seeming ability to have stopped the clock. His nut-brown hair, while shorter these days, was tousled as it always had been, inviting feminine fingers to brush it lovingly off his forehead. She could remember him thrusting his fingers through the crisp waves as he puzzled over a particularly vexing problem.

His lean face—all planes and hollows—was rugged rather than scholarly, but his green eyes revealed an intelligence that more than one magazine had described as brilliance. As those clear eyes flickered over her, Brooke felt as if she had been instantly and thoroughly summed up.

The blue oxford-cloth shirt, worn under a burgundy and gray tweed sport coat, bore water stains, causing Brooke to glance out the window to see if it had begun to rain. No, the California sun was shining as brightly as it had been when she left for work this morning.

Brooke put the puzzle of Donovan's soaked clothing from her mind as her gaze moved to his kelly-green tie. Not only was the color bright enough to startle a person, it appeared to have been trampled by a herd of rampaging elephants. His khaki slacks, although bearing the same signs of water damage as his shirt, were surprisingly well pressed. Her lips curved in a reminiscent smile as she viewed his feet.

"Is there any special reason why you're wearing one brown shoe and one black one?"

He glanced down. "I hadn't noticed."

Brooke had often considered that part of Donovan's undeniable charm was that he stimulated a woman's maternal instincts. As well as others, just as basic, she recalled. Soft color drifted into her cheeks at the memory. Feeling the warmth, she shook her head to discourage such erotic fantasies.

"I don't suppose you noticed that your shirt and slacks are wet, either."

"So they are." He appeared honestly surprised at the revelation. "The sprinklers must have been on when I came across Marston Quad."

Of course, Donovan wouldn't have noticed anything as mundane as sprinklers, Brooke considered with an odd feeling of déjà vu. Not if he had been thinking about his work.

"Why don't you sit down and tell me about your research," she suggested, gesturing toward the visitor's chair and taking her own seat.

He had forgotten she was so delicate. The huge executive chair practically swallowed her up. Despite her height, Donovan had no doubt that he could still circle her wrist with his fingers and have room to spare. Her waist was still wasp slim; he had to fight the urge to span the distance with his fingertips.

"Nice office," he commented, not quite knowing how to begin such a vital conversation. He'd rehearsed his speech for weeks, but seeing Brooke again had promptly expunged all those carefully chosen words from his mind.

Her almond-shaped eyes moved around the room. "At least it has a window. With all the overcrowding, I was warned not to expect even that."

Upon her arrival last week at the Althea D. Smiley Coeducational College, better known simply as Smiley College, Brooke had been assigned space on the first floor of the Carnegie Building. While not much bigger than a broom closet, the office did come equipped with the indefatigable Mrs. Harrigan, a definite bonus in anyone's book.

After taking one look at her small office, Brooke had made the immediate decision to redecorate as soon as her busy schedule allowed. Despite the fact that the college budget did not make provision for more than a can of paint, Brooke was willing to supply both the material and the labor to convert her office into something more suitable. As it was, the tobacco-brown rug, chunky oak furniture and black leather upholstery reminded her of a stuffy old men's club. All she needed was a humidor of fat cigars on her desk and a couple of trophy heads mounted on the wall. A soft gray blue would be nice for the walls, she had decided. Cherry furniture, a few plants, and she would begin to feel at home.

Home. This campus had been her home for four of the most challenging, exciting years of her life. The last two of those years had been spent with the man sitting across the wide desk from her now. Brooke sighed to herself, wondering vaguely whether Thomas Wolfe might not have been right, after all. Unwilling to consider that her return to the college could be a disastrous mistake, Brooke forced her mind back to the matter at hand.

"Unfortunately, I can only give you ten minutes, Donovan. I had blocked out half an hour in my appointment book but..." Her voice trailed off and she merely shrugged.

"I was late," Donovan finished good-naturedly. "As your bully of a receptionist felt moved to point out."

"She's not a bully," Brooke argued. "She simply takes her work seriously."

"If you were seeking to present an intimidating first impression, Brooke, you've definitely pulled it off with that granite-faced gorgon. The woman reminds me of the fire-breathing dragon who guards the treasure in all those video quest games.''

A reluctant smile quirked at the corners of her lips. ''Shame on you. How do you think poor Mrs. Harrigan would feel if she knew she had just been compared to a dragon?''

''Harrigan?'' Donovan flashed a bold, self-assured grin. ''Piece of cake,'' he murmured, more to himself than to her.

''Excuse me?''

He leaned back in the chair and crossed his arms, appearing more than a little pleased with himself. ''Don't you think that a Kincaid and a Harrigan might find a little common ground? Luck of the Irish, and all that.''

Past experience had taught Brooke to distrust Donovan when he pulled out that smooth Irish charm. It had always been a fascinating dichotomy of his nature that the man could totally ignore her existence for days, then suddenly appear at her door, flowers in hand, a small obscure book of poetry or some other specially chosen present in the back pocket of his jeans and a picnic hamper brimming with irresistible gourmet treats in his sporty yellow MG. On cue, she had succumbed each and every time.

''I don't remember you believing in luck,'' she said coolly.

His smile faded as he met her suddenly challenging gaze. ''You've a good memory.''

Unfortunately that was proving all too true. Brooke was more than a little shaken by the way this meeting had brought back the past in such vivid detail.

''Tell me about your work,'' she instructed.

Her crisp, businesslike tone was something new. Alien. Donovan wasn't certain that he liked it. He found himself undeniably unsettled by the idea of dealing with the sleek executive Brooke had become. Her tailored ivory silk suit was a long way from the tight jeans he remembered so fondly. A quick glance at her hands indicated that she had quit biting her nails. The absence of a wedding ring revealed that she had not remarried, but Donovan knew that. The moment he had discovered that Brooke had been hired, he'd used his winning smile with the secretary in personnel to gain access to her résumé.

When he had first heard of her marriage to a Bay area stockbroker, Donovan had experienced a jolt of jealousy so strong that it shook him to the core. After her divorce, he'd been forced to wonder how there could be two men in the world foolish enough to let Brooke Stirling get away.

"Why don't we discuss it over dinner," he coaxed. "Since I can't really do my project justice in ten minutes." He glanced down at his watch. "Eight," he corrected. "And counting."

Irritation rose as old resentments, feelings Brooke had thought she had overcome years earlier, came surging to the surface. Her tawny eyes hardened to agate.

"It isn't my fault that you got so tied up in your work that you kept me waiting for twenty minutes," she flared. "If you wanted to talk me into releasing funds for your precious project, Donovan, you should have shown me the consideration of arriving on time."

If he was surprised by Brooke's sudden display of temper, Donovan failed to show it. Instead he eyed her dispassionately. "This conversation sounds vaguely familiar."

Despite the fact that she had quit smoking over three years ago, Brooke found herself desperately wanting a cigarette. Needing something to do with her hands, she picked up a slender gold pen.

"I'm surprised you recall any of our conversations," she replied, forcing an uncaring tone as she toyed with the pen. "Especially since I was never certain whether or not you were listening to a single word I said."

"Oh, I was listening all right."

Brooke opted not to attempt to discern the reason for the odd grievance suddenly thickening his tone. "How nice to have that little matter cleared up after all these years," she said briskly. She gripped the pen tighter as her trembling hands threatened to reveal how distressed she was by the turn this conversation had taken.

Donovan didn't miss the whitening of Brooke's knuckles, the slight rise in the timbre of her voice. So, she wasn't as in control as she would like him to believe. He found it reassuring that she was no more comfortable with this situation than he was.

"How about visiting the Coop?" he suggested suddenly. "I'll buy you a double malted. It'll be just like old times."

She had twisted the pen apart. They both watched, momentarily distracted, as the spring hit the blotter before bouncing off the desk to land several feet away on the dark carpeting.

"I haven't had a double malted in years," Brooke said at length.

"You have been living a deprived existence, haven't you?"

It was the smile that served to strengthen her resolve. It was too boyishly charming, too alluring. He'd always been able to get his way by flashing that damn smile.

That was all it had taken to get her to forgive him, time and time again.

Not this time, she vowed. While it was obvious that Donovan had not changed one iota in all their years apart, she most certainly had. And she was not foolhardy enough to get involved with a man whose primary interest in life was his work.

"My life is none of your business," she snapped. "You're down to six minutes."

"Be reasonable, Brooke," Donovan protested, his own irritation beginning to rise. "I can't possibly detail years of work in a few lousy minutes."

"It's you who needs to be reasonable," she countered. "You're not the only professor on campus who has a request into this office for additional funding. Neither are you the only one with a busy schedule. The others have managed to present themselves in my office at their appointed hours, describing their work succinctly in the allotted time. Why should you receive special privileges?"

"Because my work is important, damn it!"

"So I remember you saying." She rose from her chair, her cool gaze belying the warm September temperature. "Your time is up, Professor Kincaid."

Realizing that it would be pointless to argue when he was so angry himself, Donovan got up out of the chair. "I never thought you'd be one to hold a grudge, Brooke."

"That's not what I'm doing."

His green eyes held quiet censure. "Isn't it?"

"I've a meeting with President Chambers, in his office, in precisely five minutes. If I don't leave now, I'll be late."

Donovan took the receiver of her desk phone from its cradle and held it out to her. "Call his secretary and reschedule."

Brooke bristled visibly. "I most certainly will not. President Chambers is an extremely busy man."

"And I'm not?"

"While I see your ego hasn't suffered one bit over the years, may I point out that you are definitely not as important as the president of the college."

Donovan had been working around the clock for the past week. During the scant time he had allowed for sleep, he had been struck with an uncharacteristic insomnia. Fatigue, concern over the continuation of his primate research program, combined with the unsettling emotions seeing Brooke again had stimulated, conspired to make his words rash.

"I can damn well remember a time when you thought differently."

Brooke shot Donovan a narrow-eyed look that assured him he had spoken out of turn. "If you don't watch it, Professor Kincaid," she warned quietly, "your little surrogate family could find itself flat out of gorilla chow."

An irritating buzz came onto the line, signaling unnecessarily that the receiver was off the hook. Donovan hung up the telephone with a deep sigh. "This isn't going to be as easy as I'd hoped," he muttered under his breath.

"Talking an old lover into giving you everything you want?" she asked acidly.

"You always did have an unfortunate tendency to jump to hasty conclusions, Brooke. If I remember correctly, I warned you that if you ever wanted to become a successful accountant, you'd have to stifle the impulsive side of your nature.''

"I've become successful enough to have been offered this position."

"So you have," Donovan agreed, rubbing his chin. Having shaved off his beard only last week, Donovan still wasn't quite used to its absence. "However," he decided after observing her for a long, thoughtful time, "I don't believe you've lost your propensity for rash behavior."

"Not that it matters, but you're dead wrong on this one, Donovan. However, since you believe I leaped to a false conclusion, why don't you explain your earlier statement about this not being as easy as you'd hoped?"

He shrugged. "I'm simply surprised to discover how uncomfortable it is attempting to discuss business with you after leaving so many personal things unsettled."

Brooke pressed her fingers against the desktop for support as she felt her knees turning to water. "We settled everything that needed to be settled," she said in a soft, not very self-assured tone.

For one brief fleeting moment, she was his Brooke. That wide-eyed, lovely young thing who had been an enticing blend of cool sophisticate and sensual seductress. Despite the fact that she had adopted what amounted to a campus uniform in those days—jeans, message T-shirts and running shoes—Brooke had not been able to camouflage the aura of restraint that was a direct result of her upbringing.

Like other young women of the era, she had been brought up by the book. However, in her case, the text that had served as Carolyn Stirling's parental bible was not Dr. Spock but Amy Vanderbilt. Brooke's manners were impeccable, and there had been those who had sworn that they had never heard her once raise her voice in either anger or excitement.

But Donovan had known better. Upon spotting her at a fraternity mixer, he had felt as if he had been struck by lightning. Fortunately for the state of his nerves, not to mention his libido, Brooke had been affected no less harshly. By the end of the first week they were lovers. As they continued to be for two long, glorious years.

There had been a time when Donovan had believed that a man could tire of limiting his amorous activities to a single woman; Brooke immediately disproved that erroneous theory. Each time they made love, it was just like the first time. Only better. There was nothing he found more exciting than releasing the passionate young gypsy who lay hidden beneath Brooke's proper, unapproachable exterior.

Brooke had given him much more than love; with her uninhibited response to his lovemaking, she had brought sunshine, fantasy and magic into his life. Until this very moment, Donovan had not realized that she had taken all those gifts with her when she left.

"I'm not sure we have," he murmured. He slipped his hands into his pockets to keep from touching her. "What are you doing after your meeting with President Chambers?"

"I'm leaving for Sacramento."

"Sacramento? You just arrived in Claremont last week."

"This offer was totally unexpected. Since I had to spend the past three weeks briefing my replacement on the governor's commission, I didn't manage to get all my things packed before I was expected to show up here for work....

"I hadn't realized you noticed I'd arrived," she tacked on quickly, taking a sudden interest in an impromptu touch football game starting up on the lawn outside her office window.

"Of course I did."

When Brooke finally returned her gaze to Donovan, her eyes were veiled with soft censure. "You didn't call."

Donovan merely shrugged, not wanting to admit the many times during the past seven days he had picked up the phone, only to put it down again. What could he have possibly said that would have changed things? Giving the matter considerable thought, even as he had tried to drown himself in his work, Donovan had come to the reluctant conclusion that there was nothing he could say or do that would undo the mistakes of the past. It was then he had vowed to keep their discussions solely on business.

Now, as he viewed Brooke's tawny-gold eyes, the soft flush staining her cheeks, the delicate line of her lips, Donovan found himself beginning to regret what might have been too hasty a decision.

"That was my mistake. I'm sorry."

She closed her eyes briefly, as if garnering strength. "You don't have to apologize."

"I think I do," Donovan insisted quietly. "For a great many things."

Brooke had to stifle the impulse to put her hands over her ears to keep from hearing any more of his enticing words. She couldn't—wouldn't—allow herself to succumb to his charms. A strident signal suddenly shattered the thick silence permeating the office, and she could have kissed her secretary for the timely interruption. Pushing the intercom button, she prayed Donovan would not observe the trembling of her fingers.

"Yes?"

"If you don't leave immediately, Ms Stirling, you'll be late for your meeting with the president." From the woman's tone, Brooke discerned that President Chambers was not that far down from the Holy Father himself when it came to Mrs. Harrigan's personal hierarchy.

"Thank you, Mrs. Harrigan. I'm just leaving."

As she brushed past Donovan, her perfume hit him like a hard right to the midsection. It wasn't a softly delicate floral, reminiscent of spring gardens, but neither was it the musky, heavy Oriental scent he remembered her mother to have favored. While decidedly feminine, the fragrance was bright, crisp and clean. It reminded him of something, but Donovan couldn't quite pinpoint exactly what.

"I'll walk you over to Sumner Hall," Donovan offered expansively as he left the building with Brooke.

Outside a coverall-clad workman was cutting the expanse of velvety green lawn in front of the auditorium, and Brooke had to raise her voice to be heard over the lawnmower.

"And give me a treatise on why you're more entitled to additional funds than the rest of your colleagues? No thanks."

Brooke tilted her face toward the expanse of clear blue sky. "The sun is shining, there's not a speck of smog in the sky, the birds are singing, and I've been locked in that cell of an office since seven o'clock this morning. I'd like to enjoy this little stroll." She waved a greeting to the postman as he peddled by on his bicycle. "Without annoying interruptions."

Donovan grimaced at her dry tone. "And I'm an annoying interruption?"

She stopped her brisk pace just long enough to inhale the sweet scent from a rosebush covered with brilliant scarlet flowers. "I always admired your perception, Donovan."

He plucked a single bud from a stem, ignoring Brooke's murmur of protest as he inserted it into the sleek dark coil at the back of her neck. "You've developed some tough armor in your metamorphosis from student to financial administrator."

Her only response was a slight shrug.

They had reached the ivy-covered brick building housing the administrative offices. As Brooke began to climb the steps, Donovan caught her arm. "I'd still like an opportunity to take you to dinner."

"Thanks, but no thanks."

To Brooke's surprise, Donovan accepted her refusal without a word of protest. "Could I at least invite you to drop by the center and see my work for yourself?"

"That's not necessary. Simply submit a proposal, like everyone else, Dr. Kincaid."

His fingers tightened. "I'm not like everyone else."

Brooke's amber eyes handed him a warning. "I'll say this for you," she said slowly, carefully, in an attempt to remain calm, "you're certainly a great deal more rude than the faculty members I've met thus far." With that she shook free, ran up the steps and disappeared behind the heavy doors.

Donovan debated following her. Then, deciding that he'd only anger her further by intruding on her meeting with the college president, he sat down on the stone steps, prepared to wait until doomsday, if that's what it took.

He shook his head as he stretched his long legs out in front of him. Brooke was right, he mused, he *was* wearing one black shoe and one brown one. Not that such behavior was so unusual; Donovan was well aware of his reputation as the quintessential absentminded professor. Funny that the description had never bothered him until now.

He sighed as he tried to recall his carefully prepared speech concerning his need for additional funding. As he rehearsed the all-important pitch under his breath, Donovan failed to notice the indulgent but decidedly inviting smiles slanted his way by more than one passing coed.

Chapter Two

Brooke fought down the unwelcome flash of pleasure she experienced as she exited the building an hour later to find Donovan sitting precisely where she had left him.

"What are you doing here?"

He rose lazily to his feet, giving her that smile she had tried so many times over the years to forget. "Waiting for you."

Her high heels clattered on the steps as she briskly walked past him. "I've already told you, Donovan, send me your proposal and I'll consider it along with the others."

"Don't I at least get special consideration for old time's sake?" he argued, his long legs having no difficulty keeping up with her.

She skidded to a halt, shading her eyes from the brilliance of the sun as she looked up at him. "If you're going to bring old times into it," she warned, "I may have to send your precious proposal through the paper shredder."

"I don't remember you being so vengeful," he chided softly.

"You were so busy with your stupid monkeys, I'm surprised you noticed anything about me," she snapped as she continued her march down the sidewalk.

"Apes."

"What?" Brooke radiated irritation.

"In those days I was working with chimpanzees," he explained with exaggerated patience. "These days my focus is gorillas. But they've always been apes, Brooke. Not monkeys."

"Whatever." She stopped at the corner of Fourth Street and College Avenue to allow a car to pass. "Just leave that proposal with Mrs. Harrigan," she instructed formally. "I'll take a look at it when I get back from Sacramento." Dismissing him with a brief nod, she turned toward the ancient Carnegie Building.

Donovan was not to be that easily deterred. "I've got a better idea," he said, taking her arm to turn her in the opposite direction.

"Donovan," Brooke complained, "let me go. I've got work to do."

"I'm only helping you with your work," he argued. "There's no way you can appreciate my proposal without seeing the subjects firsthand."

"I'm not interested," she muttered, remembering all those hours spent standing idly by as Donovan had struggled to communicate with his stupid monkeys. Apes, she corrected mentally.

"Besides," he added, as if sharing the very same thoughts, "on a personal note, I'd like you to see how far my work has come since our undergraduate days."

"I've read all about your research in *National Geographic*. Not to mention *Time* and *Newsweek*. The press, at least, appears quite impressed with your work."

"But you're not."

Brooke didn't answer, instead stopping to watch a hummingbird hover over a scarlet hibiscus. She loved the lush green parklike grounds of the college. The woods at the far edge of the campus held particularly evocative memories. Memories she knew she was far better off ignoring.

"Remember the afternoon we made love in the woods?" Donovan asked suddenly.

Brooke didn't dare look at him. "Vaguely," she lied. She could remember every sensual, exciting detail. "I seem to recall being scared to death that someone would come along and catch us."

"I'll admit now that I was as afraid of detection as you were. But it didn't stop us from taking the chance."

"No," Brooke admitted reluctantly. "It didn't. But we were both crazy in those days."

"Crazy in love, perhaps," he corrected quietly. "Ah, the impetuousness of youth." He smiled at the shared memory. "God, you were beautiful, your slim girlish body bathed in the gold and claret glow of the sunset."

Donovan eyed the elaborate twist at the back of her neck with scant appreciation. "You were wearing your hair simpler in those days. It was long. And straight."

She had been able to sit on it. Lord, how he had loved to spend lazy moonlit hours arranging those dark silken strands over her taut young breasts!

"I ironed it."

His lips tilted upward. "I remember. I also remember the time you fried the ends."

"You wouldn't stop kissing my neck," she accused. "It was all your fault I forgot what I was doing."

"I stopped before you burned it off at the scalp," he countered. His expression turned thoughtful. "Perhaps that was my mistake."

"What?"

"Stopping. If I'd kept you in my bed, you wouldn't have gotten wanderlust."

"Me?" She stared up at him. "I think you're forgetting precisely who jilted whom here, Donovan Kincaid!"

His jaw hardened. "I'll admit to making a mistake when I ungallantly rejected your unexpected, rather vague business proposal. But that doesn't mean that I didn't feel like hell, leaving for New York without you."

You couldn't have felt as bad as I did, Brooke could have answered. She wisely held her tongue.

"It's not right to use your personal feelings for me as an excuse to sabotage my research, Brooke," Donovan said quietly.

Annoyance flared in her eyes. Despite her high heels, Brooke had to tilt her head back to glare up at him. The idea that Donovan's lofty height gave him a distinct confrontational advantage infuriated her.

"If I visit your zoo, will you promise to let me make my decision in peace?"

She could talk as coolly as she liked, but judging by the fire in her eyes, she hadn't lost all of her passion. Donovan welcomed Brooke's anger. It made her more accessible.

His expression turned apologetic. "I can't agree to that. This project means too much to me."

"So what else is new," she muttered.

An uncomfortable silence settled between them as they continued to walk down the tree-lined sidewalk. Brooke shook her head, wondering what had made her think she could return to work at the same college where she had foolishly fallen in love with the brilliant but otherwise committed young scientist.

Upon receiving the offer from the board of regents last month, Brooke had assured herself, during several long pep-talk sessions, that she was an adult woman, with a vital, active career, capable of handling anything. Including working with a former lover.

After having graduated with a degree in accounting, and being jilted by Donovan Kincaid, Brooke had taken a position with a small but promising computer firm in the heart of what would become known as the Silicon Valley. Neither of the owners of the company could boast a college education, but both were geniuses in the new and growing field of computers.

Within five whirlwind years, Brooke found herself heading a twenty-person accounting department. Despite her hectic work schedule, she managed to attend nearby Stanford at night, earning both her M.B.A. and C.P.A.

During that same period of time, she married a successful young stockbroker. Her mother, who had openly disapproved of the vague young student Brooke had brought home from time to time, was thrilled by her daughter's marriage to such a prize catch. Three years later, when the ill-fated marriage had ended in an amiable enough divorce, Carolyn Stirling had taken to her bed for a week. Despite the fact that their divorce had been as politely dispassionate as their marriage, Brooke could not deny that the experience had hurt her deeply.

Failure was always painful, she reminded herself now. Perhaps that was why she was finding this enforced reunion with Donovan so disquieting.

Although she had proven a washout when it came to romantic relationships, at least Brooke could take comfort in the fact that she had proven herself adept at her work. When she had reluctantly approached the owners of the company with the news that she was leaving to open her own accounting firm five years ago, they had not only wished her well, but sent her enough referrals to allow her to finish her first year in the black. Four years later she had been both surprised and flattered to receive an offer to join the governor's task force on public funding.

In turn, her high profile and success on the committee had brought her full circle, back to where she had begun. Confident in her ability, Brooke refused to believe her appointment had anything to do with the fact that one of her ancestors had founded the college.

As Appropriations Director for the small but prestigious liberal arts college thirty-five miles east of Los Angeles, it was Brooke's responsibility to examine the funding of various research projects. She was to select those individuals whose work was deserving of continued financial support, while paring down the operating budgets of other ongoing projects. If she were actually as vengeful as Donovan had accused, it was well within her power to literally destroy his life's work. Something she would never do.

However the unpleasant fact remained that she would probably have to drastically reduce Donovan's funds. With the cutback in federal grants, there was only so much money available. From what she had seen of the budget requests so far, he was in for some very stiff competition.

"It's not much farther," he said, misunderstanding her soft sigh.

How could she forget? Brooke was dismayed to realize that she could find her way to the primate center blindfolded, even after all these years.

Despite her vow to remain personally disinterested in Donovan's research, Brooke secretly marveled as he put his beloved gorillas through their paces. He truly loved them, she realized as he informed the group of his approach with a deep belch. At her poorly hidden look of surprise, Donovan explained the odd sound to be one of *Gorilla gorilla beringei*'s signals.

The next hour flew by as Brooke was introduced to members of Donovan's extended gorilla family. She oohed and aahed over the infant, Toto, who, presently suckling tranquilly at his mother's breast, appeared unconcerned about Brooke's appearance in the compound. As Donovan explained the giant apes' dietary preferences, Brooke found herself accepting a branch of foliage from Auntie Em.

"What do you know about that," Donovan enthused. "As a rule, Auntie Em is uniquely selfish, totally ignoring the concept of their group. I've never seen her share her food with anyone."

"I suppose I should feel honored," Brooke murmured, absently placing the branch on a nearby metal table.

Brooke stifled a scream as Auntie Em chose that precise moment to violently throw herself at the bars with the full weight of her three-hundred-plus pounds. As the gorilla's excited cries echoed around them, Brooke immediately backed away.

"What on earth is the matter with her?"

Donovan appeared blithely unconcerned by the huge black ape's behavior. "Auntie Em likes you," he explained conversationally. "She simply wants to share."

"I took her branch," Brooke pointed out. "What else does she expect me to do?"

"She wants you to eat the leaves."

Brooke stared at him in disbelief. "You have got to be kidding."

Before he could answer, Auntie Em picked up a tire and flung it across the compound, where it hit Long John Silver, the sleeping old patriarch of the family.

"I'd suggest you take a bite, Brooke," Donovan said calmly. "Before things erupt into a full-scale riot in there."

When Toto, disturbed by the commotion, began to screech, his mother rose and moved threateningly toward Auntie Em, who in turn began flinging handfuls of fruit peelings at the advancing ape. A total uproar appeared to be moments away.

"All right!" Brooke grabbed the branch, stripped off a couple of leaves and dutifully shoved them into her mouth.

Fortunately the action had the desired effect. Auntie Em's lips immediately curled back to display huge yellow teeth in a broad grin. She sat back down on the ground and stripped her own branch, happily stuffing handfuls of the dark green leaves into her mouth. Toto's mother returned to her corner, where she once again made soft cooing sounds to her offspring. The old silverback, appearing relieved the commotion was over, closed his eyes and fell back to sleep. His rumbling snores resembled a volcano about to erupt.

Still having difficulty believing what she had just done, Brooke attempted to convince herself that the green leaves weren't so terribly different from the spinach fettuccine she'd eaten last night for dinner.

"If the other women you bring to this place are forced to eat foliage, you must be a real fun date."

"Auntie Em has never offered food to anyone else," Donovan said casually, as if he didn't find anything the slightest bit odd in the sight of Brooke chewing on eucalyptus leaves. "Come on, I'll introduce you to Gloria."

Shaking her head with a combination of frustration and reluctant laughter, Brooke followed Donovan around the corner, where she came across a huge female gorilla whose dark eyes were glued to a wide-screen television. At the present time, *Miami Vice*'s dapper detective Sonny Crockett was rattling off an incomprehensible command in Japanese.

"Gloria's got a satellite dish that picks up signals from all over the world," Donovan explained. "Once I began letting her change her own channels, I discovered she has a definite yen for police shows."

Without warning, the picture began to roll. "Uh-oh," Donovan muttered. "Here we go again."

They were forced to stand by helplessly as Gloria hooted her irritation while punching the buttons of the channel selector in a futile attempt to locate another, steadier signal. The screen suddenly went dark. In a display of viewer rage, the gorilla flung the control across the compound and began beating her fists frantically against her chest. Belatedly spying Donovan, Gloria's hands began moving in rapid, precise movements.

"Is she doing what I think she is?" Brooke asked, stunned by the idea that this enormous animal was actually communicating with Donovan.

"She's signing," he agreed, his own hands flashing in response to the gorilla's frantic hand signals.

"I've read about that," Brooke admitted. "Although I've never quite believed it was possible. Don't I remember you telling me that only chimps could be taught to sign?"

"Not only was I a philistine in those days, I was a closed-minded one," he admitted with a self-deprecating grin. "But in my defense, I was only parroting what all the experts used to say.

"In fact, when you and I were going to school here, the general consensus of opinion was that chimpanzees were capable of conceptualization and abstraction beyond the abilities of a gorilla. Gloria, along with a handful of other test subjects, has rewritten the textbooks."

Brooke could hear the unmistakable pride in Donovan's voice and decided that he was deserving of it. "What's she saying?"

"She wants me to fix her television." His hands moved fluidly as he answered the gorilla.

Gloria's dark face radiated displeasure as she gave a series of jerky, obviously derisive gestures.

"Now what?" Brooke asked.

"I told her I couldn't. Actually," Donovan said as an aside to Brooke, "the repairman told me three months ago that the set was on its last legs. Anyway, Gloria isn't exactly pleased with my refusal. She called me a bad, dirty pig." He eyed her for a moment, taking in another series of brusque hand gestures. "And a rat. And an ugly snake."

Donovan's own fingers flashed in response to the gorilla epithets, and Brooke had the uneasy feeling that she had been brought into this conversation when the ape's flashing dark eyes settled on her. Showing her teeth, Gloria turned her conversational skills Brooke's way.

"She says hello," Donovan translated.

"How do I answer?"

"She can understand spoken conversation," he explained, "but it helps to back up your words with signs."

Brooke watched as Donovan signed a greeting. A moment later she repeated it to Gloria, whose grin widened appreciatively. The gorilla circled her dark face with a wide hand.

"She says you're beautiful," Donovan told Brooke. "Like a pretty flower."

"How nice," Brooke enthused, conveniently putting aside the idea that if anyone had told her a few days ago that she'd be having this conversation with a gorilla, she'd have declared them certifiable. "What's the sign for thank you?"

After Donovan demonstrated, Brooke tried to duplicate the gesture. She decided that she must have been successful when her effort earned another complicated, lengthy flare of hands.

"She loves you very much and wants you to come see her every day."

"Thank you." Brooke said the words aloud as she signed them. This time the gesture felt more natural. She grinned up at Donovan. "Why do I suspect you rehearsed all this in order to get on my good side?"

He shook his head. "We didn't rehearse a thing, Brooke. The compliments were all Gloria's idea." His eyes gleamed with devilish lights. "Although I'll have to admit that she found you a great deal more interesting once I explained that you were the one in charge of getting her a new television.''

"A what?" Stunned, Brooke stared up at him.

Before Donovan could answer, a chase scene from *The Streets of San Francisco* appeared on the screen. As the huge ape sat back down to watch, it was as if her temper tantrum had never occurred.

"Did you ever think that Gloria's disposition might be improved by a visit to Mr. Rogers' neighborhood?" Brooke's disbelieving gaze moved back and forth between the now placated gorilla and Michael Douglas and Karl Malden carrying on a heated argument in Italian.

"I tried that," Donovan admitted. "But it didn't work. Gloria has very definite tastes and if she isn't allowed to watch her favorite shows, she digs in her heels and refuses to work on the language experiments."

His expression was a mixture of parental pride and researcher frustration as he studied Gloria thoughtfully. "She's perpetrating a form of emotional blackmail far more sophisticated than usually documented by other studies of her species."

Despite her dislike of corporal punishment, Brooke personally thought that Gloria needed a good spanking. The only problem, she admitted, was finding someone to administer that needed solution. While Gloria's behavior might resemble that of a spoiled child, she outweighed the average preschooler by at least two hundred pounds.

"You've definitely got your work cut out for you, Donovan. Gloria is a long way from trying to teach Curly hand signals."

His expression brightened. "You remembered him."

"How could I not, since I saw as much of those chimps as I did you? I remember them all—Curly, Mo, Harpo."

"Don't forget Groucho. He was the first one to sign your name."

Brooke wondered if any woman had ever had a more unorthodox courtship. If she and Donovan *had* actually gotten married, she wouldn't have been at all surprised if he had insisted on taking the family of chimpanzees along on their honeymoon.

"I suppose part of your grant request is going to include a repair call for that television." Brooke wondered how she was ever going to explain that to the board. Though she was, in theory, in charge of appropriations, she needed the board of regents' approval for all cash disbursements.

"I'm asking more than that," Donovan admitted reluctantly. "I need a replacement, Brooke."

"A replacement large-screen television set for a gorilla? Give me a break here, Donovan."

He frowned. "It's an invaluable learning tool."

Brooke crossed her arms over her chest. "One of these days, Professor Kincaid, you should climb down from your ivory tower long enough to check out some of the television sets around this campus," she suggested dryly. "One dorm finally managed to get a replacement for their twelve-inch black and white last year. Believe me, the board will never approve such a frivolous expenditure."

"Then you'll just have to convince them, won't you?"

"First you'll have to convince me," she countered.

"That's what I intend to do," he said mildly. "Over dinner."

Donovan's gaze held not a sign of guile from what she could see. But Brooke reminded herself that she had been fooled before by those bright emerald eyes.

"I'm not having dinner with you, Donovan."

"Is that final?"

She nodded firmly. "Carved in stone."

He eyed her thoughtfully. "You know, when we were going to school here, I was convinced that you were the most intelligent, beautiful girl on campus."

She arched an argumentative brow. "And now?"

"Now although you're obviously still intelligent and more beautiful than ever, you're also about as stubborn as a damn trail mule."

"Or a *Gorilla gorilla beringei.*"

He smiled at the comparison. "Got it." He looped a friendly arm around her shoulder as they left the center.

"Don't," Brooke protested, shaking free of the casual embrace. "People will talk."

Sunshine, he realized suddenly, pinpointing the scent of her perfume. Brooke smelled like the bright gold of a noonday sun reflecting off the water of some icy wooded alpine lake. At that irrational comparison, Donovan struggled to come up with a reason for these fanciful thoughts he'd been having lately. Overwork, he assured himself. That's all it was.

"Let them." His voice was entirely too low, too alluring.

"Donovan," Brooke protested, "if this is some ploy to convince me to give you the funds, you're going about it in the wrong way."

"After the way you've screwed up my work, you owe me the courtesy of hearing me out," he argued.

"*I've* screwed up your work? I wasn't the one who failed to show up on time for our meeting today, Donovan. As it was, I was forced to reschedule you three times this week because you kept calling Mrs. Harrigan with one flimsy excuse after another why you couldn't keep your appointment. If you ask me, your cavalier behavior hasn't demonstrated a great deal of concern over your proposed financing."

"Damn the money." His fingers cupped her chin, holding her when she would have turned away. "Do you know how much I've thought about you lately?" A low vibrating anger thickened his tone. His intelligent green eyes were narrow slits.

"Do you know how much sleep I've lost? How many research notes I've misplaced while my mind is spinning fantasies of you? Of the alluring sunshine scent of your perfume. The satin of your skin. The sweet taste of your lips."

There was an intensity to his voice that made Brooke's pulse thud a little wildly. "I've only been in Claremont one week," she argued. "Seven sleepless nights don't exactly earn you a spot in the *Guinness Book of World Records*, Professor Kincaid."

Donovan bit back an oath as he shook his head, firmly, decisively. "It's been longer than that. I haven't been able to get you out of my mind since July."

"July? You couldn't have known I was coming here in July. My appointment was a last-minute decision when the man pegged for the spot decided to accept a more lucrative offer from an international bank in Hong Kong."

"I didn't know you were coming," Donovan agreed grimly. If he had, all this would at least make more sense.

"Then why—"

"It's a long story." He shaped her shoulders coaxingly with his palms. "Let me explain it to you over dinner."

"I really do have a plane to catch," she insisted, cautiously retreating.

Donovan eyed her with obvious regret. "I don't remember you being so cruel, Brooke," he said quietly.

"I'm not cruel."

"Aren't you? How else can you explain the fact that you've denied me even a simple, harmless little hello kiss?"

By the time he lowered his head, Brooke believed herself prepared for Donovan's kiss. As his lips touched hers with the impact of a live wire, she was to be proven wrong. Never could she have been prepared for the blinding flash of lights that exploded behind her eyelids; it would have been inconceivable to expect her head to spin dizzily as he traced her parted lips with the tip of his tongue. And there was no way she could have predicted the sheer, unadulterated thrill that coursed through her veins as Donovan's mouth increased its pressure on hers. There had never been any simple, harmless kisses from this man. Why had she thought it would be any different this time?

Fire. As it scorched through him, Donovan belatedly realized that he had badly miscalculated. He had planned nothing more than an exploratory kiss. A kiss for old time's sake, out of curiosity, to see if the flame of passion had managed to remain alight all these years. He had not been prepared for the hunger that rose, hot and unrestrained, to sear at the very core of his self-restraint. Her mouth was as soft, as tender as it had been in the dreams that had tortured him last night, but so much warmer. How could he have forgotten this heat?

Her slender body, as she willingly allowed him to draw her into his embrace, was a contradiction of strength and delicacy that had him yearning to rip off the proper silk suit and experience the sheer pleasure of her lying underneath him, flesh to flesh, her woman to his man.

He tilted his head back, releasing her mouth just long enough to drink in the sight of her flushed complexion. In the soft twilight glow, her skin reminded him of apricot satin.

"Nice," he murmured, running his finger down the side of her face.

Over the years Brooke had learned to keep her impulsive nature on a tight leash. Accountants known for their rash behavior did not attract many clients. Morning after morning, year after year, she had slipped into her aura of cool sophistication right along with her tailored suits, having discovered early in her career that donning a mask of cool competence actually helped her feel like the person she was pretending to be.

As his lips plucked teasingly, enticingly, at hers, Brooke's vow to keep her relationship with Donovan on a strictly business basis disintegrated like dry leaves under the gale-force winds of a hurricane.

"Better than nice," she whispered.

"Much better," Donovan agreed roughly.

His mouth roved her uplifted face, scattering kisses across her cheeks, her eyelids, her chin, the bridge of her nose. Hunger—hotter and more virulent than anything he had ever known—ripped through him.

"Let's try it again," he murmured. "Simply for experimental purposes, of course."

She went up on her toes, twining her arms around his neck. "Yes."

As he took her mouth in an all-consuming kiss, effervescent pleasure bubbled up inside Brooke, sparkling and golden, like champagne. Donovan's kiss was everything she had remembered, and more, so very much more. And his hands, as they roved her back under her suit jacket, were what she had been missing in a man's touch.

"Come home with me." His words were a hot breeze against her neck.

Brooke closed her eyes to the pleasure of his palm stroking her breast through the dark gold silk of her blouse. "I can't."

"Of course you can." Donovan could feel the tremors running through her. Violent waves that were echoed deep within his own body. "Nothing's changed between us, Brooke." His fingers dug into her hips as he urged her against his stirring rigidity. "Feel what you've done to me," he rasped. "You could always make me want you with a single look. A touch. Remember?"

Remember? How could she have forgotten? The passion she had experienced with Donovan Kincaid had been like nothing she had ever known, before or since. He had taken her to the very heights of ecstasy from the beginning. And in the end, Donovan had taught her a very basic lesson in human anatomy. No one had ever died from a broken heart.

"That's enough." She dragged her lips from his.

Through the fire scorching his mind, Donovan felt the slight pressure of Brooke's hands against his shoulders at the same time he was deprived of the sweet glory of her avid mouth. Slowly, reluctantly, he tilted his head back to gaze down into her face.

Her tawny eyes were still filled with unmistakable desire, but there was a hint of apprehension in their golden depths, as well. Was she afraid that he would force his physical advantage and make love to her, here and now?

Not that he wouldn't want to, Donovan considered. God, she was beautiful! He was finding it amazing that Brooke was even lovelier in real life than she had appeared in those tormenting fantasies these past two months since London. Ever since he had witnessed the short-lived disaster between Serena and Alex during the Wimbledon fortnight.

Donovan had spent much of last spring semester on the sidelines, interestedly observing the odd-couple relationship developing between his stepsister, Serena Lawrence—known to most of the world as the "Ice Princess" of professional tennis—and Alex Bedare, former diplomat turned professor. The fact that they had struck sparks off each other from the beginning was obvious. Still, it was months before Serena had allowed those sparks to develop into a blazing inferno.

She had fought Alex's seduction attempts every inch of the way. Then, once they had become lovers, she had refused to acknowledge that anything permanent could possibly come of a relationship with a man who in earlier eras could only charitably be described as a rake. That reluctance on her part to believe in Alex had almost cost her the man she loved.

The breakup had been explosive, tempers flaring, harsh words exchanged. Donovan had been forced to stand by helplessly, offering whatever comfort he could as he waited for the lead players in the romantic melodrama to come to their senses. Come to their senses they did, reconciling under the silvery slant of London rain. The following day Serena had gone on to score an impressive Wimbledon victory.

That was all it was, he decided. The stormy courtship between his sister and new brother-in-law had simply triggered memories of his own unsuccessful love affair. Donovan felt a great deal better knowing there was a logical reason for the uncharacteristic thoughts of Brooke he had been suffering lately.

"It was good, Brooke," he reminded her gruffly as he framed her face between his palms. "It could be good again." The pulse at the base of her throat beat strongly as Donovan's thumb grazed it. "It *will* be good again," he vowed.

Brooke backed away, praying that she would be able to stand unassisted. Her legs felt like jelly and her head was still fogged with unsatiated desire.

"Your methods won't work these days," she insisted in a voice that she wished desperately was stronger. More assertive. "I'm not going to sleep with you, Donovan. So you may as well give up on that lobbying idea."

His temper rose, but Donovan controlled it. "At least let me take you to the airport," he said reasonably.

Suspicious of his sudden easygoing attitude, Brooke searched his face for some inkling of his thoughts. Nothing.

"No," she said. Then, hating the weakness apparent in the soft sound, she strengthened her tone as well as her resolve. "No."

"Wouldn't you like some company into L.A.?"

"Really, it's not necessary. Besides, I'm not flying out of LAX; my plane leaves from the Ontario airport. It's only a ten-minute drive from my apartment to the terminal."

"Where are you living?"

"The Cloisters." She grimaced at the thought of her disorderly apartment. "Although living is a relative term: surviving would probably describe circumstances better. I've been so busy trying to wade my way through all the proposals, that I still haven't had time to unpack.''

The Cloisters suited her, he thought. Secluded behind private entry walls, the condominium apartments offered spectacular views of the San Bernardino Mountains. While Donovan had never been privileged enough to enter those guarded gates, he had heard rumors of sumptuous marble baths, circular staircases and indoor fountains. Thinking of his own small, cozy Edwardian home, he was forced, not for the first time, to compare Brooke's background with his own.

The only child of a wealthy bank president and a woman whose family had made a fortune by subdividing practically the entire San Fernando Valley, Brooke had been born with the proverbial silver spoon in one hand and a fistful of gold charge cards in the other. Her parents, ecstatic when blessed with a golden-eyed infant in their later years, had never denied Brooke anything, that Donovan could see. He had no doubt that her income from various trust funds was several times his annual salary at the college.

Donovan could not even boast an impoverished, colorful past. He came from a solid middle-class background, of which he was the first in a long line of Kincaids to attend college, let alone receive a doctoral degree and some measure of international fame.

However, despite his admitted success, there were instances—and this was decidedly one of them—that Donovan was reminded all too clearly of those few times he had been a guest at Brooke's family's palatial estate. While her mother would have eaten her Gucci handbags before permitting herself to be rude, Carolyn Stirling had, with a brief glance, a murmured statement, made Donovan well aware of the fact that he and Brooke came from two entirely different worlds.

Donovan refused to allow himself to dwell on negative thoughts. "When will you be back?"

"The day after tomorrow. I only have a few last things to pack. Some books, photo albums, that sort of thing. Why?"

He shrugged. "Just idle curiosity."

Her sober eyes handed him a warning. "I won't have made up my mind about your project by then, Donovan."

Irritation flared, fierce and uninvited. Donovan shoved his hands into his pockets to keep from shaking her. "I wasn't asking about the project, Brooke."

Something in his tone alerted her to the fact that he was telling the truth. She repeated her question. "Then why were you asking?"

He gave her a totally innocent, totally false smile. "Can't a man ask a simple question without getting the third degree?"

Brooke stared at him, intently studying his face once again as she tried to read some secret message in his inscrutable expression.

"I have a plane to catch," she said finally.

"To Sacramento," he agreed. "We'll talk when you get back."

"About work," she warned.

"Of course." He bent his head, pressing his lips against hers for a quick, hard kiss. "Have a safe flight." He brushed his knuckles down her cheek. "I'll see you Saturday."

Donovan let her get a few feet away before he spoke. "Oh, Brooke?"

She turned slowly, viewing the devils dancing in his green eyes with very real trepidation. "Yes?"

"If all I wanted was to sleep with you for old time's sake, sweetheart, you would have spent this evening sharing my bed instead of cramped in a narrow seat on a plane to Sacramento."

With that he turned, sauntering off in the opposite direction. Brooke remained rooted to the spot, her eyes glued to his back as she pressed her fingertips experimentally against her lips where she could still feel the warmth generated by his kiss.

Chapter Three

Late Saturday afternoon Donovan was standing in the doorway of Brooke's office, allowing himself the pleasure of observing her undetected. Of all the views Southern California had to offer, he decided that this was undeniably his favorite.

Let the surfers have the crashing waves and sparkling sands of Zuma and Huntington beaches. The movie stars could claim the smog-free air and sprawling estates of Beverly Hills and Bel Air, while their kiddies lived it up at Disneyland or Knotts Berry Farm. Weekend skiers were welcome to those purple-hazed mountains, which would soon be wearing a winter dusting of snow, just minutes from campus.

Given his choice of all those natural and man-made wonders, Donovan would choose this sight of Brooke, down on her hands and knees, laboriously sanding the wood floor, every time. The denim shorts rode high on her hips, exposing long, smooth legs that were tanned to a hue only shades lighter than the wood she was laboring over.

As desire swelled up inside him, Donovan knew that he was going to have to make love to Brooke again. It was either that or spend the rest of his life able to think of nothing else.

"You know, they have machines to do that," he said finally.

Her shoulders tensed almost imperceptibly as Brooke looked up to view Donovan leaning lazily against the doorframe. She had been surprised by exactly how much she had missed him during her time in Sacramento. Surprised and disturbed.

She didn't want to like him; she didn't want to feel as if the sun had cut through the layers of smog every time he smiled at her. And dear Lord, she certainly hadn't invited those sensual dreams that had disturbed her sleep ever since experiencing that mind-blinding kiss.

She sat back on her heels, returning her gaze to the floor. "I know. But they can scratch the wood."

"Why don't you just get a new rug?" Donovan glanced over at the one she had rolled up and dragged out into the hallway. "Not that there was anything wrong with the old one."

"The old one was brown," she said, as if that explained everything.

"I see," Donovan answered, not seeing anything at all.

But she was looking too enticing to waste time discussing the state of old rugs and weathered floors. The red T-shirt hugged curves that were fuller than he remembered. But every bit as enticing. Her hips, clad in the snug cut-offs, swelled outward from a slender waist. And those long shapely legs. The fantasies inspired by those legs were probably against the law in at least thirty-seven states.

"You sure don't look like the Director of Appropriations today," he said after the leisurely examination.

Brooke wanted to sink through the parquet flooring as she felt a warm flush color her cheeks. Thirty-three years old and still blushing. What on earth would he think of her?

"More like the janitor, right?"

"No," he said slowly, decisively, "more like a sexy, young coed I used to know."

"That was a long time ago, Donovan."

He sat down beside her, toying with the long, dark braid hanging down her back. "So you keep telling me."

"I'll keep telling you until you finally listen to reason," Brooke insisted. "What we had was nothing more than a college romance. No different from hundreds of others. Thousands."

"You never could lie, Brooke. Your face gives you away every time."

She had tied the thick braid with a piece of scarlet ribbon, leaving a fan of silky chestnut hair that Donovan brushed with a teasing, tantalizing touch over her cheek and down her throat.

"What we had was special."

"I don't remember you taking the time to notice," she argued weakly.

"My fault entirely," he agreed without hesitation. His eyes remained locked on hers as he tugged on the ribbon. A moment later it was lying on the newly sanded floor. "I've been giving the matter a great deal of thought recently."

Brooke told herself that she should insist he stop twining his fingers through the braid as he unwound it from the bottom upward. But she couldn't find the words.

"Oh?" Trying for an air of unconcern, she failed miserably.

"I ignored you." Appearing fascinated with the intricate French braiding, Donovan traced the weaving with his fingertip. "For the chimps."

"You ignored me," Brooke agreed in an attempt to remind her rebellious body of the fact that she had every reason to hate Donovan Kincaid. So why did she feel as if a live wire was thrumming through her every time he got near her?

Having freed her hair from the braid, Donovan lifted soft clouds of it over her shoulders. "That's better," he murmured.

The heels of his hands brushed against the soft slope of her breasts as he arranged the silken strands to his liking, but if Donovan took notice of Brooke's sharp intake of breath, he failed to mention it.

"I'm not going to make the same mistakes this time, Brooke."

She couldn't—wouldn't—meet his intense gaze. Instead Brooke shot a quick glance at the wall clock hanging above the door. "Just look at the time!" Shaking free of his light touch, she jumped to her feet. "I have to get home."

Donovan rose from the floor as well. "Why?"

She refused to admit she was running away from him. "I've plans for the evening."

That much was true. She had intended to spend a long, leisurely evening soaking her aching body in a bubble bath. Then, after indulging herself with a thick, gooey, take-out pizza with everything on it, she had planned to pass the remainder of the Saturday night with a horror novel she bought months ago and had yet to find the time to read.

"Have dinner with me instead," he suggested.

Brooke shook her head. "I can't do that."

His grin was beguiling, coaxing acquiescence. "Sure you can. It's easy. Just call the guy, whoever he is, and tell him something's come up."

The blithe way he suggested she lie to another individual, albeit an imaginary person, just so that she could spend the evening with him reminded Brooke that to Donovan, the world always revolved around his wishes. His plans.

"I won't do that," she said impatiently. "Now, if you don't mind, I'd like to lock up my office."

Donovan was more than a little disgruntled by her refusal. It wasn't as if he was desperate for her company tonight. In fact, if Brooke had stayed in Sacramento an additional day, he would have spent the evening with Gloria, working on the computer language program he was developing. If he was willing to forgo his work, why couldn't she cancel her damn date?

"You're not being fair about this, Brooke," he argued as they left the office. "After all, I've offered to give up my work tonight to take you to dinner. The least you could do would be to appreciate it."

Brooke shook her head as she locked the door. Then she patted his cheek. "I wouldn't want you to give up your work on my account, Donovan. Gracious, I'd spend the entire evening feeling guilty."

With that she turned away, walking down the hallway without a backward glance. Despite the fact that a slow, simmering frustration burned deep inside him, Donovan couldn't help noticing that she looked every bit as good in those raggedy cutoffs as she had in her undergraduate days. His irritation with her behavior was overcome by a sharp jolt of desire. Donovan couldn't

remember wanting a woman as badly as he wanted
Brooke Stirling at this moment.

Unfortunately—and this was turning out to be a
shock—the feeling appeared to be one-sided. He wondered who she was seeing this evening, then decided it
didn't matter. Donovan hated the guy, whoever he was.
Muttering a low oath, he turned and strode off in the
opposite direction, determined to put the frustrating
woman out of his mind.

Four hours later, Donovan learned what he had already suspected: forgetting Brooke was easier said than
done. His work turned out to be a total wash as his
imagination conjured up scenes of Brooke on her date,
laughing, dancing, sharing low intimate conversation
over a candlelight dinner. When he began picturing her
making slow, passionate love with some faceless rival,
his temper exploded and he yelled at Gloria, which in
turn hurt the ultrasensitive gorilla's feelings.

"Donovan mean," the synthetic, feminine computer
voice announced as Gloria typed the message onto the
keyboard in a unique hunt-and-peck fashion. "Donovan bad. Bad devil. Rat."

After a lengthy string of such colorful epithets, she
finished with the worst insult in her lexicon. "Ugly alli-
gator," the artificial voice accused. Glaring at him furiously, Gloria stuck out her tongue before turning away
from the computer keyboard to begin watching television.

"It's just as well we're calling it a night," Donovan
muttered, rummaging through a filing cabinet for the
bottle of Scotch he had stashed there. "The mood I'm
in, any words I teach you would get edited from any
reputable scientific journal for obscenity reasons."

He eyed the insults still blinking on the screen, the green phosphorus letters bright against the black background. "No point in encouraging you, since you're naturally a foulmouthed woman, anyway."

Donovan found himself wishing that Serena and Alex weren't out of town visiting friends. It would be nice to have someone to talk to about all this. Fortunately the semester was scheduled to begin in just a few days; Alex would have to return for his classes. Perhaps by then there wouldn't even be a problem to discuss.

Heaving a frustrated sigh, Donovan poured a drink and sat down with the giant ape to watch *Baretta* in German.

While Donovan struggled with his feelings for Brooke, she was having no better luck ignoring their situation. She had indulged in the luxury of the bath, as well as the pizza. But as much as she had been looking forward to reading Colin Tiernan's latest blockbuster, *Nighthawk*, she found she couldn't keep her mind on the story. Her eyes kept drifting to her desk, where Donovan's proposal lay.

Finally giving up, she placed the book in the drawer of her night table. Sitting down at the desk, she pulled out a scratch pad and began making notations. The replacement television for Gloria was obviously out of the question. Brooke drew a line through the figure Donovan had quoted. Even if she were to approve the purchase, there was no way the board of regents would go along with it.

There had been a steady cutback in federal funding over the years and although the college had been successful in luring corporate sponsors into the fold, it was an unpleasant fact that the budget was shrinking day by day. Everyone needed to economize—from the students who found their tuition raised for the third time in three years, to the college employees whose salaries had been temporarily frozen, to the professors who, along with the rest of the academic community, would simply have to tighten their belts.

It was Brooke's job to make everyone concerned understand that the days of freewheeling spending were gone; that they all had to make sacrifices. And Gloria, she decided, would have to suffer right along with everyone else.

She tapped her pencil absently on the pad as she continued to read through Donovan's well-written proposal. Although understanding his desire for a mate for Gloria, enabling the gorilla to teach her offspring what she had learned, there were simply no funds available to feed and house another *Gorilla gorilla beringei*, even if they were able to locate a zoo or primate center willing to lend them an adult male.

Besides, Donovan's records showed that he had brought in a male from the Cornell primate center this past spring. Apparently, according to his sketchy report of the incident, not only had Gloria steadfastly rejected her potential suitor, she had given him a black eye and a broken jaw as well. Brooke drew a line through that figure as well. Gloria would simply have to remain celibate for another year.

That left her with the language studies. Brooke chewed on the end of the pencil as she carefully studied Donovan's detailed description of his work. It was undeniably fascinating.

Gloria was obviously intelligent, despite her lowbrow choice in television programming. Donovan had monitored her IQ from the time she was three years old. At that time she scored about average for a child of the same age. Over the past five years, her scores had remained consistent with the average human population.

When using Ameslan, the American Sign Language, Gloria was proficient in some twelve hundred signs and used nearly six hundred regularly. Since moving to the computer and voice synthesizer, she had intensified her ability to communicate abstract ideas and feelings.

Even while Brooke was intrigued with Donovan's work with Gloria, the business side of her nature was able to view the potential rewards of his research. Not only would the findings increase the scientific community's knowledge of all primates, man included, but there were hopes that eventually the research could be applied to teaching humans disabled in communications, as well as preserving the endangered gorilla in the wild.

As noble as those ventures were, they were also cut from the fabric of which important awards were given. The more recognition and plaudits Donovan's work earned, the more prestige garnered by the college. And that, she knew, translated directly into contribution dollars.

Brooke smiled as she wrote *approved* in the margin next to Donovan's request for continued funding for Gloria's language studies. Then she went to bed, where she spent the night dreaming of Donovan. They were dancing to soft, romantic music on a deserted beach, the sky a vast canopy of stars overhead. It was a magical night, filled with possibilities. The entire scenario would have been absolutely perfect if only Gloria could have been made to stop cutting in.

Early the following morning Brooke was back at her office, transforming the small room with a lot of elbow grease and several cans of paint. By the time she decided to call it a day, the muddy-brown walls were a soft biscayne-blue and the extensive woodwork, including the molding along the high ceiling, was gleaming with white enamel. Every bone in her body ached from the unaccustomed physical labor, but as she walked to the parking lot, she felt as if she had accomplished something. Unlike her work as Appropriations Director, which these days had her feeling as if she were running on a treadmill.

"Damn." Brooke's frustrated sigh feathered her bangs as she twisted the key in the ignition of her late model Mercedes convertible sports car once again. Her only answer was an ominous click.

"It's your battery."

At the familiar voice, she glanced up, not particularly surprised to see Donovan standing beside the car. She had been expecting him to show up at the office all day.

"It can't be," she argued, turning the key once more. "I bought a new one last month."

"What time did you drive over here this morning?"

Brooke felt like cursing when the engine consistently refused to turn over. "Six. I had a lot to do; I wanted to get an early start. What does that have to do with anything?"

"I was just thinking that you may have left your lights on," he offered helpfully.

Brooke glanced down at the dashboard. Terrific. That's precisely what she'd done. "Since when are you so good at remembering the mundane little details of everyday life?" she snapped, angry with herself for being so stupid.

"Since I did it myself three times last week," Donovan returned easily, not appearing at all affronted by her irritated tone. "Why don't you come over to my house? It's not far from here."

She drummed her fingers impatiently on the steering wheel as she tried to decide what to do. "Your house? Why?"

"You can use my phone to call the motor club," he explained patiently. "They'll come out and recharge it for you."

"I can also use the phone in my office."

He gave her a slow, coaxing smile. "Ah, but do you have a pitcher of lemonade in your office?"

"Damn you, Donovan Kincaid." Brooke's exasperated breath feathered the hair from her eyes. "You really don't fight fair."

He reached down and opened the car door. "I didn't realize we were fighting."

"Aren't we?" she asked, plucking her purse from the front seat.

Donovan considered that for a moment. "Nope. I don't think so," he said finally. "At least I'm not." He looked down at her curiously. "Are you?"

As his green eyes held hers, Brooke was awash in sensual stimuli. Her fingers itched to brush away a tumbled brown wave that dipped over his forehead. Just as her hands ached to frame his face and her lips yearned to press against his smiling ones.

"Not today," she answered. It was little more than a whisper, but Donovan had heard it just the same.

The dazzling smile moved to his eyes. "I'm glad."

"I'm looking forward to seeing how you live, Donovan," she said as they walked the short distance to his house. "Ever since the seventh grade, when I stayed up all night reading Mary Shelley's *Frankenstein* by flashlight under the covers, I've been utterly fascinated by you mad scientist types. Do you all conduct dark and mysterious experiments in your basement laboratories?''

She was babbling. Brooke knew she was, but desperate for a safe, noncontroversial subject, she seemed unable to stop herself. Only a moment ago, she had felt as if she were being drawn deeper and deeper into the warm tourmaline depths of Donovan's eyes.

She was a grown woman with a successful career. She had survived a marriage that should have been declared terminal at the altar. Over the years, she had certainly not suffered from a dearth of male companionship, although she had always been careful to keep her relationships casual.

Brooke lived alone, traveled alone and liked it that way just fine, thank you. She was a totally independent woman. So why did she continually feel like a foolish, prattling schoolgirl whenever she was around Donovan Kincaid?

"I'll try not to disillusion you," Donovan said amiably. "Although I suppose I should warn you ahead of time that my house doesn't boast a basement laboratory."

"How disappointing."

"But it does possess a pair of cupolas. And a tower room that was obviously designed for hiding away insane relatives."

She nodded her satisfaction. "That's much better. There just may be hope for you yet, Professor Kincaid."

His smile was warm, but unthreatening. "That's what I've been telling you."

When he took Brooke's hand as they crossed Harvard Avenue, she could not deny that she enjoyed the feel of his long fingers laced together with hers. Reminding herself that one thing she didn't need was another complication in her life, Brooke immediately put the evocative sensation from her mind, instead turning the conversation to his work.

"I reread your proposal last night."

He glanced down at her curiously. "I thought you had a date."

Brooke reminded herself that one of the reasons she never lied was that she was no good at it. As Donovan had already accurately pointed out.

"I did. I read the proposal after I returned home."

Donovan had the distinct impression that Brooke was not telling the truth. That she had spent a lonely evening at home, just as he had. And if she had been with another man, the guy obviously hadn't spent the night. Even a woman as dedicated to her work as he suspected Brooke was these days, wouldn't crawl out of a passion-warmed bed to read some admittedly dry, boring grant proposal. He fought down his surge of satisfaction, not wanting Brooke to discern how pleased he was with the idea of her spending the night thinking of him.

"What did you think?" he asked noncommittally.

"It was interesting," she hedged.

Donovan warned himself to keep his tone casual, even when every nerve in his body was on red alert. He couldn't imagine not getting the funds he had requested. After all, his work was important. Brooke was an intelligent woman; surely she'd see the potential in his projects.

"Does that mean I'm going to get the money?"

She frowned. "Donovan, you know I can't tell you that. You'll have to wait until the official announcement, along with everyone else."

"Damn it, Brooke, that isn't fair!"

She tilted her chin as she met his frustrated gaze. "Actually, it is fair, Professor Kincaid. To everyone. Even someone with Gloria's IQ could see that."

By bringing up his pet project, Brooke had effectively turned Donovan's ire to enthusiasm. "Her actual score's a lot higher than she tests. The problem is that the tests are prejudiced against gorillas."

She smiled faintly. "It's hard to believe anyone would go out of their way to purposely make a test that's prejudiced against apes."

Her sunshine scent teased his senses as he walked beside her down the ivy-edged sidewalk. Donovan valiantly tried to keep up his end of the conversation as a slow, treacherous desire curled its way outward from the pit of his stomach.

"There's a definite cultural bias toward humans," he insisted. "For example, let's say that you were asked to pick two things that were good to eat. The suggested objects were a chair, a flower, a banana and a steak. What would you choose?"

"I'd choose the banana and the steak, of course," Brooke answered promptly, beginning to get Donovan's drift. "But Gloria, being a gorilla—"

"Picked the banana and the flower," Donovan finished for her. "Here's another. Where would you want to live? In a car, a table, a house or a tree?"

"Gloria chose the tree."

"Exactly. Unfortunately, the rules for scoring the test required that I record those answers as errors."

Brooke eyed him with uncensored admiration. "Your work with her is fascinating, Donovan."

"Fascinating enough to write me a check?" At her glower, he immediately lifted his hands. "Okay, I won't ask again."

"Good."

"Of course, you're always free to volunteer whatever information your little heart desires," he said with a broad, encouraging smile.

"You're pushing," she warned.

Donovan sighed. "I know. But it's important to me, Brooke. I just want you to understand that."

Remembering his attitude twelve years ago, Brooke felt that she understood all too well how importantly Donovan viewed his work. It had literally consumed his every waking moment and many that he should have spent sleeping. From his behavior since her arrival in Claremont, Brooke discerned that if anything, the passage of time had only increased his dedication. Any woman would be foolhardy to get involved with a man whose life revolved around his work. To be burned twice, by the very same individual, would be the absolute height of folly.

"Here we are," Donovan announced, stopping in front of his small Edwardian house.

As Brooke viewed the bright blue siding and wide front porch, she fell totally, irreversibly, in love. "It's marvelous." She ran up the steps. "It reminds me of a dollhouse. Oh, Donovan, I absolutely adore it."

He hadn't been aware of the fact that he was holding his breath, waiting for her opinion, until he released it on a deep sigh of relief. As Brooke sank happily down onto the blue and white pillows of the porch swing, his eyes created optical illusions, framing her in the center of his vision, blurring everything around her like a camera with a short depth of field.

Her long legs, as she stretched them out in front of her, appeared to go on forever. Her T-shirt hugged curves that he ached to touch and Donovan knew that were he to draw closer, her scintillant scent would envelop him in a soft, sensual cloud.

Despite the desire battering away inside him, Donovan managed to keep his tone light. "Even if it doesn't look like an appropriate lair for a mad scientist?"

Brooke was looking up at the striped awning, admiring the jaunty white fringe. At Donovan's question, she turned her attention toward him and began rocking slightly as she considered his words.

"Perhaps there really is a flesh-and-blood man living inside that single-minded scientist, after all," she mused.

"I believe that's one of the points I've been trying to make," he said quietly.

Did he know what he was doing to her? Did he realize that when he looked at her that way he made her feel need, whether she wanted to or not?

"Among others. Let's not forget your work," she replied, fighting the urge to open her arms to him.

"Let's," he countered, his expression suddenly unnervingly sober. "I promised myself that I wouldn't make the same mistakes this time, Brooke. I'm not going to ignore you. I'm not going to worry about the differences in our backgrounds. What I should or shouldn't do. Instead, I'm going to do what I know is right for both of us. What we need. And, whether you'll admit it or not, want."

Brooke didn't try to deny his words. She knew there was no need. "How long am I to be given your undivided attention, Donovan?" she challenged softly. "Five minutes? Ten?"

"All evening," he answered huskily. "Hell, all night. I want you, Brooke. I want you back in my arms again. I want to touch you, taste you, watch your eyes darken

with passion, hear the soft little sounds you make when
I pleasure you.''

As Donovan sought to convince Brooke that their
lovemaking was as right as it was inevitable, he found his
words to be a form of masochistic self-torture. Desire
clawed at his insides.

''And then, in the morning, I want to wake you up in
the same way, loving you as you were meant to be
loved.''

If Brooke was shaken by his words, by the hunger that
flared in his eyes, she was even more distressed by her
own answering response. Sparks skittered over her skin,
flames licked at her blood, making her feel as if she were
on the verge of spontaneous combustion.

Despite a career based on the ability for clear, rational thought, Brooke could not be dispassionate about
her feelings. While Donovan treated everything, including his personal life, as a scientific problem to be re-
solved step by logical step, she tended to rely on her
instincts. And right now her instincts were telling her
that everything was happening too soon. She needed
more time.

''While that's a nice little scenario you've painted, it
isn't going to happen.'' Brooke wondered whom she was
trying harder to convince, Donovan or herself. ''I'm
going to use your telephone to call the motor club and
after my car is running, I'm going straight home.''

She might be able to postpone what was going to
happen, Donovan admitted grimly, but she wasn't going to stop it. ''Are you certain that's what you really
want?''

At this precise moment, Brooke wasn't sure of anything. ''Very certain,'' she said steadily. Her heart was
beating like a jackhammer.

"Fine," Donovan agreed, ignoring the knot of need twisting his stomach as he fought to keep his tone casual.

But as he began searching for the house key he'd hidden under one of the clay pots lining the generous railing of the front porch, his hands were not as steady as they might have been.

Chapter Four

The motor club promised to send a man out within the hour. Now all Brooke had to do was survive the wait.

"You know," Donovan said softly, "we're going to have to talk about it."

"Talk about what?" she asked distractedly, her gaze moving around the room.

When they had been students at the college, Donovan's dormitory room had always looked as if a tornado had swept through it. Obviously his housekeeping skills hadn't changed. Books and papers were strewn over every flat surface, including the floor.

His expression was strangely serious as their eyes met. "Our breakup. And how it affected our lives."

"My life is none of your concern, Donovan. As for my asking you to marry me, chalk it up to a young girl's folly."

Dragging her gaze from those brilliant green eyes, Brooke picked up a piece of fool's gold masquerading as a paperweight on Donovan's cluttered desk. Her fingers traced a sparkling vein. "Actually, I'd forgotten all about it until you brought it up the other day," she murmured.

Donovan frowned. "Really?"

Unprepared to meet his eyes again quite yet, especially after telling such an outrageous falsehood, Brooke put the paperweight back on the desk and picked up a thick textbook.

"Really," she insisted as she leafed through the pages of unintelligible text. "Do you actually read this stuff?"

"That *stuff* just happens to be the definitive study of rival warfare between chimpanzees. I'm sorry."

She returned the book to the desk. "For what?"

"For behaving like such an ass. I've already admitted that I was in my self-centered stage back in those days."

His expression was unnervingly solemn, triggering a spontaneous physical pull in Brooke that was every bit as strong as it was unwelcome. She forced a cool, uncaring tone.

"And what stage are you in these days?"

The sensual mood was effectively shattered. Donovan managed a self-disparaging smile. "Apparently my poor host stage. Make yourself at home while I get that lemonade I promised you."

As soon as he had escaped to the privacy of the kitchen, Donovan sank down into a chair at the table, shaking his head in disbelief. What on earth was the matter with him? It was hard to believe that the man who had been behaving like a tongue-tied, bumbling adolescent in the other room was completely comfortable reading a scientific paper in front of an audience of five hundred individuals, at least four hundred of whom could admittedly be regarded as skeptics.

But who would have ever expected Brooke Stirling to suddenly turn up at the very same college where they had fallen in love? And how could he have foreseen that he would find her even more appealing, more desirable, than she had been during their often tempestuous love affair?

Over the past two months Donovan's memory had been playing cruel tricks on him. Brooke's low voice had murmured in his ears at the most inopportune times, and when he was supposed to be concentrating on his work he found himself recalling the way her eyes could darken to a deep, molten gold with passion. His body ached with the very real need to make love to her again after all these years.

Despite his reluctant willingness to give Brooke time to realize the inevitability of their relationship, Donovan vowed that he was going to have her. Soon, very soon, Brooke would be sharing his bed. Then perhaps he could get back to work, free of the distracting thoughts that had brought Gloria's language experiments nearly to a halt.

While Donovan strengthened his resolve in the kitchen, Brooke was utilizing her time alone to do precisely the same thing. She was not that surprised to rediscover a sensual side to her nature that she had thought successfully suppressed. Donovan always had been able to instill erotic feelings within her. Their lovemaking had been exhilarating, taking them to the heights of passion. Still, she reminded herself now, outside of Donovan's rumpled bed, all intimacy had ceased to exist. His first love had been his work. Why should she believe that he had changed?

As she thought back to that fatal day she had shown up at the lab, suggesting in an offhanded way that she accompany him to Ithaca, New York, where he had been accepted into the Cornell graduate program, Brooke was forced to admit to some small culpability in what had followed. She had not told Donovan that she loved him or that she couldn't contemplate a future without him. They had never discussed love and Brooke's pride refused to allow her to say the word first. Instead, she remembered grimly, she had presented her arguments in a rational manner that she had hoped would appeal to him.

As a married student, he would receive a larger housing allowance from the college. She'd be able to work, contributing to their finances. Well aware of Donovan's penurious financial status—her mother had derided his rented tuxedo at every opportunity—Brooke had then played her trump card. As a married couple, they'd save several hundred dollars each year on income taxes.

When Donovan had rejected her well-thought-out arguments, Brooke had promptly thrown in the towel. Two weeks later they had both graduated and gone off in different directions—Donovan to New York, Brooke to Silicon Valley. She wondered what might have happened if she had not allowed false pride to stand in her way of true happiness. If she had followed Donovan to Cornell, would they have eventually married, despite his misgivings? Would they have a family?

Shaking her head, Brooke reminded herself that she had never been the type to dwell on might-have-beens and this was definitely no time to start.

"How about some music?" Donovan asked as he returned to the living room.

"That would be nice," Brooke murmured as she accepted the tall glass Donovan handed her. "Thanks." She turned in surprise as the lyrics from *The Mikado* filled the room. "You still listen to Gilbert and Sullivan?"

"Of course." Gathering up the scattered notebooks and texts from the couch, he invited her to sit down, taking the spot beside her. "How about you?"

"I'm still a closet operetta fan," she admitted. "And Gilbert and Sullivan are my favorite. I've always loved the way Gilbert's satire matches Sullivan's sense of parody."

"Exactly." Donovan gave Brooke a rewarding look that suggested she had just discovered the secret of relativity, single-handedly. "Although they made an excellent team, you can't ignore the fact that it was Sullivan's resourceful musicianship that earned them lasting international acclaim. There's an almost mathematical purity to his scoring."

A frown formed between Brooke's brows. She vaguely recalled having this argument before. "I have to disagree with you, Donovan. It was Gilbert's verbal ingenuity that made their collaborative works special." As if to prove her point, she quoted the inscription on the Gilbert Memorial in London. "'His foe was folly and his weapon wit.'"

Donovan stretched his long legs out in front of him, eyeing his navy-blue running shoes with satisfaction. Before leaving the house this afternoon, he had double-checked to make certain his shoes had matched. Any woman who was so particular about the color of her office rug would undoubtedly prefer a lover who was consistent in his choice of footwear.

"Gilbert's plots bordered on the absurd," he argued. "Don't forget that Sullivan refused to work with him for a time for that very reason."

Brooke bit down on an ice cube, experiencing a cooling rush. "Going out on his own was one of the dumbest things Sullivan ever did. His solo works certainly don't possess the lasting quality of the operettas he scored for Gilbert.''

"You don't consider 'Onward, Christian Soldiers' a lasting song?" he questioned disbelievingly.

"Oh, that." Brooke blithely waved Donovan's argument away with a flick of her wrist. "I'll admit that one has hung around for a time, although you can't honestly believe that it even comes close to the snappy cadence inspired by Gilbert's lyrics from *The Mikado*."

"Forgive me if I fail to find 'Oh willow, titwillow, titwillow' inspiring."

Brooke's eyes shot angry sparks. "That's not fair, Donovan Kincaid, you're quoting out of context. When you sing the entire verse, it's quite pleasing."

Donovan leaped on her words. "Aha," he said triumphantly. "May I point out that you just stated that you need to *sing* the verse. So you do admit Gilbert's romanticized words are nothing without Sullivan's music."

"That's not at all what I meant," Brooke said. "And it's unfair of you to back me into a corner that way."

His expression was absolutely guileless, but Brooke could see the bold light of victory in his eyes. "Are you accusing me of using unfair debating tactics?"

"I'm accusing you of not appreciating the written word unless it's being used to describe the behavioral habits of big, hairy apes."

Donovan leaned forward, pressing his finger against her lips. "Shh," he warned, "don't let Gloria hear you say that. She's very sensitive." A grin quirked at the corners of his mouth. "For a big, hairy ape, that is."

She never could resist that teasing, boyish smile. Brooke's laughing eyes met his. "I'll try my best to avoid hurting Gloria's delicate feelings."

He nodded, satisfied. "That's better." Her lips parted instinctively as Donovan's thumb brushed across them. "I suppose Gilbert's lyrics did contribute something to their success," he allowed huskily.

She fought against the thrill his feathery touch instilled. "And Sullivan's scoring did help considerably."

"You know, we've had this argument before." He lowered his head, ever so slightly.

"I thought we had," Brooke said, backing away.

"Do you remember how we settled it last time?"

She swallowed as his gleaming, emerald eyes lifted from her mouth to smile into hers. "Not really."

"When it started, we were lying in that old beanbag chair I kept in my sitting room at the dorm." His thumb continued to trace the full line of her lips, creating havoc to her senses. "After a while, one of us—I can't remember whether it was you or me—suggested moving it to the bedroom."

Brooke struggled against the desire that was threatening to overwhelm her. "Do you happen to recall who won?"

Donovan's eyes were dark, kindled with lambent passion as they drank in her gleaming, chestnut hair, the tawny sunshine hue of her complexion, the slightly feline slant of her amber eyes. When his gaze returned to her lips, lingering on them with unspoken purpose, Brooke's heart trebled its already erratic beat.

He cupped her chin with his fingers, tilting her head back as he brushed his lips over her cheek. "I'm not certain. But I think we both did," he murmured.

His mouth covered hers quickly, unhesitatingly, drawing Brooke into a swirling realm of heat and fire before she could resist. His hands tangled in her hair, his fingers splayed against the back of her dark head in order to disallow her escape. But Brooke had no thought of retreat. Swept by a reckless desire, she clung to him, her lips opening on a soft moan, inviting further intimacies.

For a time, Donovan made love to her solely with his lips, moving them over her cheeks, her eyelids, her temples, her throat. Brooke reveled in the glorious kisses even as they made her head swim and her body ache for more. Finally, unable to remain passive any longer, she wound her arms around his neck and pressed her mouth against his in a fiery primal passion that drew a deep groan from the depths of his chest.

Donovan pressed her back against the cushions, his hands delving under the soft cotton of her aquamarine T-shirt to caress her warm, silky skin. Brooke's heart hammered against her ribs as his strong fingers reacquainted themselves with her body and she arched against him, silently urging him on as her lips continued to answer kisses that had grown almost savage in their hunger.

Her breasts were small and firm in his hands, the nipples hardening in response to the stroking touch of his fingers. Her breath grew shallow as he trailed his palm across her rib cage, down her abdomen, slipping his fingers into the waistband of her cutoffs. She was everything he remembered her to be. And more.

Brooke's body burned with a thousand flickering flames as she writhed under Donovan's increasingly intimate touch. When a small voice of reason tried to make itself known in the far reaches of her mind, she steadfastly ignored it, preferring to give herself up to the pleasure of his exquisite lovemaking. Her fingers fumbled with the buttons on his shirt, finally meeting with success as she was able to press her palms against the rigid line of his chest.

He was taut and lean, possessing the build of a long-distance runner. The fact that his body was as firm, as hard, as it had been in his youth revealed that Donovan applied the same rigid self-discipline to his physical conditioning as he did to his work.

Brooke pressed her lips against his moist skin, feeling it burn under her butterfly kisses. Even as his shuddering breath demonstrated his own struggle for control, Donovan continued to torment her, leading her further and further into the blazing inferno. She cried out as he trailed his fingers up the soft bare skin of her inner thigh, creating a pleasure just this side of pain. When his palm cupped the throbbing center of her passion, she arched against him, frustrated by the stiff barrier of denim.

His mouth was dampening the lace covering her breasts, his teasing tongue causing havoc to her senses. "You see," he murmured huskily as he plucked at the ultrasensitive tip straining beneath the gossamer fabric, "we belong together, you and I. We always have. Nothing's changed."

His fingers moved to the snap at her waist as Brooke struggled to comprehend his words through the wildfire licking at her mind. At the sound of the metal zipper slowly being lowered, she managed to decode one damning statement. *Nothing's changed.*

Her hands covered his. "No."

Donovan looked down at her flushed face. A storm continued to swirl in his eyes as he studied her slowly, intensely.

"I think you mean that."

Even as her body cried out for his continued touch, Brooke forced her mind to answer coherently. "I do. I never meant for things to get so out of hand, Donovan. I'm sorry."

You're sorry, he thought harshly. Reminding himself that nothing permanent was ever accomplished by force, Donovan fought down a surge of unreasonable anger. He prided himself on his self-control even as he managed a wry smile.

"Don't feel the need to apologize, Brooke. After all, it's the lady's prerogative to change her mind."

Not quite trusting his easy acquiescence, Brooke nevertheless breathed a silent sigh of relief as Donovan allowed her to sit up. A steady click-click sound infiltrated its way into her consciousness, indicating that the record had come to the end. Grateful for a reason to escape the intimacy of their situation, Brooke pushed herself up from the sofa and made her way across the room.

"How about *H.M.S. Pinafore*?" she suggested with feigned brightness as she flipped through the stack of record albums.

Donovan bit back a sharp response as he fought the frustration instilled by her maddening calm. Only moments ago Brooke had practically begged him to make love to her. It didn't matter that she had failed to express those feelings in words; her hands, fluttering over his body, her lips, trembling beneath his, her eyes, molten gold with passion—all these were proof enough. Now she was behaving as if they were nothing more than strangers. Or casual acquaintances. Damn her.

"'Things are seldom what they seem,'" he quoted grimly from her proposed selection.

Brooke stiffened. He had hit just a bit too close to the mark with that one. "I assume that means yes."

Donovan wasn't averse to playing games, if that's what it took to get Brooke to open up. But it seemed to him it was a damned waste of time. They were both adults; they'd been lovers for two years, the chemistry between them was undeniably still there. So what the hell was her problem?

"It means what it means," he answered obliquely. He glanced out the window at the red pickup truck pulling up in front of the house. "The motor club guy is here. Give me your key and I'll show him where your car is parked."

"Really, Donovan," Brooke protested, putting down the record album, "you've done enough. I'll go back to my car with the repairman and drive home as soon as he's finished charging the battery."

Donovan didn't budge. "Frightened, Brooke?"

She tossed her head. "Of you? Never." *Of myself, yes,* she refrained from saying.

"I'll make a deal with you."

Brooke eyed him suspiciously as she crossed her arms over her breasts. "Why do I feel like Snow White being offered a shiny red apple by the wicked stepmother?"

Donovan flung his hand against his chest. "Are you accusing me of being untrustworthy?"

"Let's just say I don't remember you being such a pouncer."

"Me? Pounce?" His smile was beguiling. It was also totally innocent and entirely feigned. "If there was any pouncing going on, Brooke, I'd say it was mutual."

Even more than what she took to be his uncaring attitude, Brooke hated the fact that Donovan was right. She'd wanted that kiss. Just as she had wanted the first one. And she knew that her resistance to him was fading with each passing day.

"There's something I want you to understand, Donovan."

He nodded obligingly, his attention momentarily drawn to the knock at the door. "As soon as I take care of your transportation problem, I'll be more than happy to listen to anything you have to say."

He held out his hand. "Now, why don't you be a nice lady and give me the key?" he suggested with a smug, masculine assurance that had Brooke all but grinding her teeth.

"For a man renowned the world over for his understanding of all the subtle nuances of primate behavior, you sure don't understand a damn thing about women, Donovan Kincaid!"

Brooke plucked her purse from a pile of test papers and marched out the door, head high, spine erect.

Donovan watched her leave, enjoying the scenery as she climbed into the cab of the motor club truck. The memory of those slender thighs pressed against his caused a renewed jolt of desire that, while not unpleasant, was decidedly frustrating. He could only hope that, like him, Brooke would return to her apartment to find her night unreasonably long, her bed unbearably lonely. He was a patient man; his work demanded it. But where Brooke was concerned, Donovan was rapidly reaching the end of his rope.

Brooke spent the next three days engrossed in her work, determined to put the maddeningly frustrating scientist from her mind. But despite a valiant effort, the task proved to be an exercise in futility. She found his face suddenly appearing on ledger sheets, swirling up from the blurring columns of dry, unexciting figures. On more than one occasion she thought she'd heard his laughter outside in the hallway, only to discover the corridor empty when she went to investigate.

Such continued behavior eventually resulted in Mrs. Harrigan beginning to eye Brooke with overt suspicion as her attention continued to wander. Finally, late Wednesday afternoon, Brooke realized that she had been reading the same memo over and over for the past hour without gleaning a single word of its purpose. She rose from her desk, figuratively throwing in the towel.

"I'll be over at the primate center if anyone calls," Brooke told her secretary, holding up a manila folder for the woman's perusal. "There are some papers Professor Kincaid needs to sign before I can continue processing his grant application."

The older woman's only response as her eyes narrowed behind the thick lenses of her spectacles was a grunted "Humph."

Knowing that she wasn't fooling Mrs. Harrigan for a moment, Brooke quickly left. When she arrived at Donovan's office in the primate center, she found a young woman hard at work correlating a stack of computer printouts.

"Professor Kincaid should be back any time," she assured Brooke helpfully. "Actually, he was due back twenty minutes ago." Her slight smile acknowledged that Donovan's concept of time was not quite the same as the rest of the working world. "I'm Stephanie Palmer, one of his teaching assistants. You're welcome to wait for him. He shouldn't be that long," she tacked on encouragingly.

Brooke glanced hesitantly around the office, which was only slightly less chaotic than Donovan's home. Stacks of textbooks and green and white computer paper lined the shelves, resembling miniature towers of

Pisa as they tilted precariously. Brooke wondered what would happen if anyone ever slammed the door. It would probably take an entire semester to sort through the resulting wreckage.

"Thank you, Stephanie," she said with an answering smile. "I think I will wait."

Stephanie obligingly whisked some papers from the seat of a chair, making room for Brooke. "Would you like some coffee? I have a class, but I could put a pot on before I go."

"I wouldn't want to make you late for your class."

"It's no problem." Her attitude was a bit too helpful, too eager.

Brooke's eyes narrowed. "Do you know who I am?"

The student's blond head bobbed. "Ms Stirling," she answered promptly. "The new Appropriations Director."

"Then Professor Kincaid has discussed his funding proposal with you?"

Again the young woman nodded. "Yes, ma'am. Of course. It's very important to all of us that Donovan, uh, Professor Kincaid, receive his funding." Her expression turned decidedly earnest. "You will approve it, won't you, Ms Stirling?"

"I'm afraid I can't comment on that at the moment."

Stephanie appeared undaunted. "I understand. Rules and all that, right?"

"That's right," Brooke agreed. "The announcement will be made after next month's board meeting."

Wide blue eyes turned sober. "I hope you're here with good news today, Ms Stirling. Professor Kincaid's really been down in the dumps lately."

Brooke had to ask. "About his funding?"

Stephanie plucked a forest-green backpack filled with books from the floor and shrugged into it. "Of course." She looked at Brooke curiously. "I mean, what else could have him so worried that he'd fall behind on Gloria's language experiments?"

"What indeed," Brooke murmured, all too aware of the fact that Donovan would never permit personal problems to interfere with his work.

"Well, 'bye," Stephanie said with a wave. "It was super meeting you, Ms Stirling."

"It was nice meeting you, Stephanie," Brooke responded, watching as the young woman left the office to be gathered up into a pair of strong masculine arms. The couple exchanged a kiss, then hand in hand headed across the campus. Brooke stifled a soft sigh at the bittersweet memories the intimate scene evoked.

Thirty minutes later, Donovan still hadn't arrived. Thinking that he might have come in the back way, Brooke left the office, entering the compound that housed the gorillas. She found Gloria watching television while chewing on a peanut butter and jelly sandwich. At Brooke's approach, the ape looked up curiously.

"Hi, Gloria," Brooke signed, pleased when Gloria returned her greeting. When the gorilla continued to sign enthusiastically, Brooke shook her head. "I'm sorry, I don't understand."

Discarding the snack with what appeared to be an almost human sigh, Gloria walked on her knuckles to the corner of her compound where the computer keyboard was located. Despite the fact that Brooke knew of the computer experiments from Donovan's proposal, it was still a bit of a shock to watch the large dark fingers tapping away at the keys.

"Donovan not here," the feminine synthesizer voice offered.

"I know," Brooke answered. "I'm waiting for him."

"Donovan bad man. He no like Gloria anymore."

"Oh, no," Brooke argued, not stopping to consider the bizarre fact that she was defending her former lover to a gorilla. "Donovan loves Gloria."

"He yell. Bad, bad words."

"He's had a lot on his mind lately."

Deep furrows marred the sloped black forehead. "What mean that?"

Brooke tried again. "Donovan's been working very hard. Sometimes he forgets to say nice things."

With an air of decidedly feminine pique, Gloria demonstrated that she was not prepared to forgive and forget quite that easily. "He say bad words," she insisted. "Him rotten smelly skunk."

"Him, uh, *he's* not really a skunk," Brooke assured the gorilla. "Just preoccupied."

"Gloria not preoccupied know."

It took Brooke a moment to decode the fractured syntax. "Busy," she explained.

This the gorilla seemed to understand. She nodded, looking at Brooke for a long, thoughtful time. Then she began flashing a rapid series of signs Brooke found incomprehensible.

"I'm sorry," Brooke reminded her. "I only know a few signs. Not nearly so many as you."

Muttering what were obviously gorilla swear words, Gloria returned to the keyboard. Brooke knew the giant ape was obviously much more comfortable with signing and appreciated the fact that she was making this extra effort to communicate.

"I know how make happy Donovan," Gloria offered. Brooke decided that if a gorilla could possess a sly smile, the one Gloria was giving her at this moment would probably fit the bill.

"How?"

"You Gloria new television buy." Gorilla teeth flashed in a broad grin. "Good idea, yes?"

Brooke found herself unreasonably affected by the hopeful glint in those ebony eyes. Still, it was not her responsibility to break the bad news to Gloria. Besides, no one was supposed to know of her decision until after the meeting of the board of regents.

Donovan certainly seemed to have surrounded himself with well-meaning lobbyists, Brooke mused. She wondered if he had trained Gloria to say these things in order to put additional pressure on her. Deciding that idea bordered on paranoia, Brooke shook her head.

"Good idea," she finally answered the waiting gorilla.

Glancing down at her watch, she realized that she was already five minutes late for her meeting with Oscar Stevenson, the longtime head of the chemistry department. Brooke had rejected the professor's first proposal as totally out of the question and now the man was back for a second try. She hoped this one would be more reasonable than his outrageously ridiculous first attempt.

"I have to go now, Gloria," she said, scribbling a quick note to Donovan asking him to give her a call. "Goodbye. It was nice visiting with you."

"Goodbye pretty lady. You soon come?"

"I'll try."

Gloria's strong dark fingers pecked out a message that was immediately echoed by the oddly mechanical female voice. "You come. You bring new television."

"I'll come," Brooke agreed, deliberately leaving out any reference to the replacement television.

As she hurried back to her office in the Carnegie Building, Brooke couldn't forget those flashing black eyes. She certainly wouldn't want to be in Donovan's shoes when it came time to inform his prodigy that she'd have to continue watching *Mod Squad* through a haze of electronic snow for yet another season.

Chapter Five

Two hours later, Brooke left her office, her work finished for the day. As she walked to the parking lot she told herself that the fact that Donovan had not responded to her hastily scribbled note was of no interest to her. None at all.

"All cooled off?"

Brooke spun around to see Donovan leaning against a palm tree. "I've no idea what you're talking about," she said stiffly, turning away to unlock the car door. "What do you do, Professor Kincaid, hang out around parking lots, hoping to pick up women?"

"After that little display of temper last Sunday, I thought it would be better to talk to you out of range of Mrs. Harrigan's beady gray eyes," he explained easily. "I wouldn't want to say anything to cause you to blow your cool, collected image in front of the dragon lady. You'll soon discover that around here, gossip travels faster than a brush fire during the Santa Ana winds.... Am I really that much of a washout when it comes to the feminine sex?"

"Let's just say you could use a few lessons." She climbed into the bucket seat, determined to drive away before he could weaken her defenses further.

Donovan was by the side of the car in two long strides, forestalling her from fastening her seat belt. "Why don't you give me a few pointers over dinner?"

"I have things to do this evening."

"Such as?"

She looked down at his hand, silently instructing him to release her. "Things."

Donovan failed to take the hint. "How can I understand the female of the species better when you insist on talking in riddles?"

"'Life's perhaps the only riddle that we shrink from giving up,'" Brooke quoted Sir W. S. Gilbert tightly as she tried to shake free of Donovan's restraining touch.

Her efforts only caused his fingers to tighten. "What the hell does that mean?"

She glared up at him. Golden eyes dueled with green for a long challenging moment. Finally realizing the ridiculousness of their situation, Brooke began to laugh.

"I don't know. But you have to admit it makes about as much sense as your crack about things not being what they seem. Now you've got me talking in song lyrics."

Donovan joined in her laughter good-naturedly, deciding that this was not the time to tell Brooke that she was dead wrong on this one. Things were not as they seemed; he could sense the intrigue flowing just beneath the surface of their relationship. And as for her quote about life being a riddle, Brooke Stirling had matured into a much more complex woman than he remembered.

"I'm only asking you to dinner, Brooke," he assured her quietly. "I promise not to ravish your delectable female body over the stuffed grape leaves. Unless you ask me to. Then, of course, I'd be forced to oblige you. It would be the only gentlemanly thing to do."

"I really have a great deal to do at home," she argued with a decided lack of conviction.

"I know a place with dynamite moussaka. In fact, it's just as good as Dimitri used to make. Except Stavros uses fried zucchini in place of the potatoes." His twinkling eyes coaxed her acquiescence. "You've really got to taste it to appreciate it. And his baklava is good enough to make the angels sing."

Brooke belatedly realized that she hadn't eaten all day. At Donovan's description of the restaurant's fare, she could feel her mouth watering. Besides, she assured herself, it would be far simpler to agree than to spend all evening arguing with him. And it had been ages since she'd had Greek food.

"With lemon honey?"

He grinned. "Is there any other way?"

Brooke sighed her surrender. "You're on. But we'll have to make it an early evening. I've got a meeting with the head of the board of regents first thing in the morning, and I want to go over my figures one last time."

"Any chance my grant proposal will be on the agenda?" he asked casually.

"You're digging again," she accused. "You know very well I can't answer that."

Actually, he was sorry he'd brought the matter up. The question had escaped his mouth before he had had time to censor his words. The one thing Donovan didn't want to do was get into another argument about their work.

"Fair enough," he said reasonably, linking his fingers with hers as she exited the car.

Brooke was frightened by the way his light touch caused her heart to beat a little faster. Why did this man have such an effect on her? Over the years she had learned to control her impulsive streak. The individuals who made up her client list expected conservatism from their accountant and she had done her very best to oblige them. But since returning to Claremont, she found herself continually tempted to permit herself one incautious, impulsive act. Her unflagging desire to make love with Donovan was staggering in its intensity.

Struck with conflicting emotions, Brooke reminded herself that it would be the height of unprofessionalism to make love to a man whose research funds depended on her acceptance of his grant proposal. In addition, try as she might, she could not put aside their past.

He had broken her heart once before. And by the way he kept attempting to learn her decision regarding his precious proposal, Brooke knew that despite his denials, Donovan hadn't really changed. His work would always come first.

She continued to remind herself of that fact as she walked with him to the restaurant in the village.

"That was absolutely delicious." Brooke sighed happily as she leaned back against the black vinyl booth. "Although I may never eat again."

Donovan grinned. "I knew you'd love this place."

Brooke's eyes swept the room. A massive mural depicting the Acropolis glowed red under a ceiling-mounted spotlight, and plastic grapevines decorated the walls. It was colorfully, wonderfully tacky. She smiled.

"It's perfect. Even better than Dimitri's. He didn't have a red light."

"Well, whatever you want to say about the atmosphere, you can't beat the food. Or the service," he said as a burly Greek appeared carrying two demitasse cups of coffee.

"So, Donovan's young lady," the owner and chef of the restaurant greeted her expansively, "what do you think of Stavros's humble cooking?"

From what she had seen of Stavros Sklavounos thus far, Brooke privately decided that there was absolutely nothing humble about the ebullient Greek. She kept that impression to herself as she gave him a dazzling smile.

"The moussaka was inspired. I've had it with eggplant in place of fried potatoes, but never zucchini."

"My mother's recipe," the man assured her, making a fleeting, automatic sign of the cross over his massive chest. "May God rest her beautiful soul."

Brooke murmured a vague agreement.

"So," Stavros said as he sat down beside her, "you approve of the moussaka. But what did you think of Stavros's salad?"

"The best I've ever eaten," she answered truthfully.

"And the baklava?"

"Donovan's right, it could make the entire host of angels sing."

Stavros visibly swelled with pride as his gaze moved finally to Brooke's dinner companion. "Your lady has good taste. So what's she doing with you?"

Donovan laughed. "Slumming, I suppose."

"I'm not his lady," Brooke felt obliged to point out since this was the second time Stavros had brought it up. It didn't escape her notice that Donovan hadn't corrected his friend.

The Greek's alert black eyes moved from Brooke to Donovan and back again. "When I was a young man in Athens, I was a *kamaki*. Do you know what that is?"

"Here it comes," Donovan groaned. "Come on, Brooke, let's get out of here before you accuse me of setting this up."

Stavros pushed Donovan back down into the black vinyl booth as easily as if he were batting at a pesky fly. "Never interrupt Stavros when he's talking to a beautiful woman."

Brooke found she rather enjoyed seeing Donovan at a disadvantage for once. The Greek was, in a word, huge. And obviously determined to finish his story.

"Please, Donovan," Brooke said, her eyes dancing as she smiled sweetly at him over the rim of her cup, "let Mr. Sklavounos go on." She turned to the restaurant proprietor. "If I remember my college mythology course correctly, a *kamaki* is a spear. The trident of Poseidon."

White teeth flashed appreciatively under a bushy, black mustache. "This one, my friend," he said to Donovan, "is no empty-headed Bobby Doll. I suggest you grab her before she gets away."

"It's Barbie Doll," Donovan corrected easily. "And you're right about her being bright. But I've already tried to grab her, Stavros, and the lady isn't buying."

"Hah!" Stavros rose from the table to tower over them, his eyes snapping. "This is the lesson I was going to tell you," he said, wagging his finger. "A *kamaki* is a young man who chases the pretty American tourist girls."

His black eyes danced with masculine appreciation as he grinned down at Brooke. "But to tell the truth, I do not remember any women as beautiful as you, lovely lady.''

"Liar," Brooke said easily. She propped her elbows on the red Formica table and rested her chin on her hands. "But I'm fascinated, nevertheless. Please continue."

Stavros switched his attention to Donovan. "This is what you must remember, my friend," he said firmly. "In order to get good results, a *kamaki* must have a mouth that runs like water. He must feel strong. How do you say it, self-assayed?"

"Self-assured," Donovan murmured.

Stavros's meaty hand waved away the correction. "Whatever," he said dismissingly. "The thing you must do is never stop. Never give up. If you're good, the girl will eventually answer. If you're very good, it will be more than a maybe."

He thrust out his barrellike chest. "It will be yes!" he roared, bellowing the acceptance to the amusement of the patrons scattered around the restaurant.

He clapped Donovan on the shoulder before taking Brooke's hand and lifting it gallantly to his lips. "If Stavros were thirty years younger, he would give Donovan a run for his money."

"I wouldn't think a good *kamaki* would let a little thing like age stand in the way," Brooke teased with a smile.

Perhaps it had been the wine, or the excellent food, but she had begun to relax during dinner. Donovan had been careful to keep the conversation light, encouraging her to forget how his uninvited presence in her life had complicated it more than she ever would have thought possible. Now, safely flirting with the outgoing

Greek restauranteur, Brooke was thoroughly enjoying herself.

"You're right," Stavros responded without missing a beat. "However, unfortunately there is always the unhappy fact that my Anna would kill me if I did anything more than look at a beautiful woman." He exhaled a huge, dramatic sigh. "She has this foolish notion that forty-five years of marriage gives her sole rights to Stavros."

Donovan laughed appreciatively. "Are you telling me that the great Stavros, one of the few self-proclaimed male chauvinists left on earth, is afraid of a mere woman?"

The old Greek gave him a pointed look that bespoke a wisdom born from a lifetime of experience. "In matters of the heart, my friend, one must always fear the female of the species."

He smiled down at Brooke. "You must come again," he instructed. "Next time leave this one at home and Stavros will demonstrate how a good *kamaki* woos a woman with mere words."

With a deep bow, he was gone. Brooke watched as he gave an effusive welcome to the couple at a neighboring table. "I like him."

Donovan tossed some bills onto the table. "I thought you might."

It was disconcerting to discover that among his other talents, Donovan appeared to possess the ability to read her so easily. "Am I that transparent?" Brooke asked as they left the small restaurant.

Donovan took a few moments to answer as they walked back to where Brooke had left her car. A harvest moon was riding upward in the sky and a few of the oak trees lining the sidewalk were wearing their fall colors of gold, crimson and orange although it would be at least another month before the landscape surrendered, albeit briefly, to the change in seasons.

"No, you're not at all transparent, Brooke," he answered finally. "I suppose I simply suspected you'd like Stavros because I like him. And I know how fond you were of Dimitri. Despite the intervening years, we still have a great deal in common."

Brooke didn't want to admit that unwelcome fact to herself. There had been too many times during dinner that the years had drifted magically away and she had felt as if she and Donovan had been transported back in time. To Dimitri's Greek restaurant in the village. Where they had gone for their first date. Where he had taken her the night they first made love.

"You're exaggerating."

"Am I?" he murmured.

He stopped, taking both her hands in his as he looked down into her face. Brooke opened her mouth to protest, but closed it again as she viewed the seriousness of his expression.

"I'm a scientist, Brooke. I never exaggerate anything; it isn't my nature to do so. I'll be the first to admit that I approach life as an experiment, a problem to be solved with the same scientific method I use in my work. Some people find that an irritating habit, but it's one I can't, and won't, change."

"Donovan," Brooke protested, becoming increasingly unnerved as his thumbs traced concentric circles on the tender skin of her palms, "this isn't necessary."

"Of course it is," he corrected quietly, firmly. "I seem to recall you taking a couple of physics classes. Do you remember the scientific method?"

"Not exactly. Donovan, I really do have to get home."

He remained unmoved by her protest. "In grossly simplistic terms," he explained slowly, "scientific method is comprised of three steps, the first being observation."

"Donovan—"

"That's the most important one; observation is the beginning and end of scientific reasoning. It must be carried out painstakingly to ensure that all the pertinent facts are collected and that each fact is checked for accuracy."

He leaned toward her. "Want to know what facts I've observed about us thus far?"

Brooke refused to allow her eyes to falter from his. "Not really."

As his hands moved to her wrists, Donovan took note of her speeded-up pulse. A very good sign. One more piece of evidence to add to the ever-growing list. "Too bad, you're going to hear them anyway. We both like Gilbert and Sullivan, Greek food, sunshine and smog-free days."

"So do millions of other individuals," Brooke pointed out.

He inclined his head. "True. It's also true that we both hate subterfuge, playing games, and unless you've changed drastically in the intervening years, dress-up Sunday brunches."

"We could probably find twenty people on this block alone who feel the same way."

The smile playing at the corners of his lips was so slight it was barely there at all. "Probably could," he agreed amiably.

Donovan lifted her hand to press a kiss against skin his touch had already warmed. "Another point in my favor," he said, watching carefully as her eyes gleamed in response. "Your pulse quickens when I touch you. Your lovely eyes darken to molten gold. And were I to give in to temptation and kiss those soft, alluring lips, you'd begin to tremble in my arms."

His voice was deep, husky with unsatiated hunger. "Admit it, Brooke, despite every ounce of common sense you possess, you want to explore this unexpected phenomenon as much as I do."

"No," she whispered, shaking her head. "I don't."

"I thought I'd warned you never to lie, Brooke," Donovan advised conversationally. "You really aren't very good at it."

Brooke welcomed the annoyance that flashed through her at his lazy self-assured tone. Her irritation showed in the sudden thrust of her chin.

"You're as egotistical as you ever were, Donovan Kincaid."

His eyes moved to her hair. She'd obviously had it cut in the last three days. The gleaming chestnut waves skimmed her shoulders as she tossed her head. Donovan brushed his knuckles over her cheek.

"And you're as irresistible as ever."

As Donovan ducked his head, Brooke decided that this little game had gone far enough. Too far, she admitted as she found herself wanting just one more of Donovan's dazzling kisses before she turned her back on this unwilling attraction.

"No," she insisted, turning her head at the last minute. When his lips brushed her cheek, Brooke felt her knees begin to melt.

"Running away again, Brooke?" Donovan inquired mildly. "I don't recall you being such a coward."

"I'm not a coward," she flared. "But I am getting fed up with your constant seduction routine. You've a good memory, Donovan, I did take a few science classes in college. And I remember very well that after observation comes generalization."

Sparks practically arced about her head as she glared up at him, hands splayed on her hips. "Well, in this case, Mr. Wizard, your generalization is all wrong. So put that in your Bunsen burner and smoke it!"

She spun around and marched away. She had spunk, Donovan considered, watching her with admiration. He'd always liked that in a woman. Just as he reluctantly appreciated the fact that Brooke wasn't going to make things easy for him. Donovan had always been suspicious of things that came too easily.

He knew that the last thing Brooke wanted right now was his company, but he wasn't about to put her at risk just to soothe her feminine pride. While Claremont admittedly wasn't Los Angeles, it still wasn't prudent behavior for a woman to be walking the streets alone at night. Slipping his hands into his pockets, he strolled after her, his long stride enabling him to catch up with her as she reached the corner.

"Go away." Brooke's angry gaze was directed toward the red Don't Walk signal as if she could change it to green with the sheer strength of her will.

"Sorry," he refused amiably. "Despite what you think of me, I'm not the type of man to allow a woman to walk home alone from a date."

"It wasn't a date," she snapped. "It was dinner. Nothing more."

"An enjoyable dinner. I think you made Stavros's evening. Do you realize that I probably won't be allowed to eat there ever again unless I take you with me? Would you really condemn a man to a life without Stavros's baklava?"

Brooke had no choice but to laugh. "Damn it, Donovan, I like you."

"You're supposed to," he said simply, taking her elbow as the light changed.

"You make it sound so easy."

"Isn't it?"

They were approaching her car now and Donovan found himself unwilling to allow the evening to end. "Do you recall what generalization leads to?" he asked casually as she dug in her purse for her keys.

"Not really." Her dismissing tone handed him a stiff warning. A warning Donovan blithely chose to ignore.

"Prediction." He plucked the keys from her fingers, dropping them into his own pocket. "Want to know my prediction about us?"

"I'm not the slightest bit interested," Brooke said firmly. "Thank you for dinner, Donovan. It was, uh, interesting. Now, if you don't mind, I'd appreciate you returning my keys."

His long fingers cupped her chin as he brushed his lips lightly, teasingly, against hers. "Not as interesting as things are going to get." His lips plucked enticingly at hers. "Don't tell me you'd really rather go home to those cold, unfeeling accounting books, when you could be sharing an after-dinner drink back at my place?"

"I have a great deal of work to do." She held out her hand for the purloined car keys.

He shook his head. "Uh-uh. I refuse to believe that you didn't have your presentation prepared at least two days ago." He eyed her thoughtfully. "Three," he decided.

Brooke's eyes widened as she looked up at him. "How did you know that?"

He sloped her shoulders with his hands, the gesture strangely comforting and exciting at the same time. "You were always prepared days in advance, sweetheart. Your note cards would be alphabetized, your bibliography completed and your paper typed up with nary an error on those pristine white pages before I'd even settled on a topic."

"You were incorrigible," Brooke said with a reminiscent smile. "I used to lie awake nights worrying that you'd never graduate."

Her softly issued words brought images slamming into his mind. They were undeniably erotic, yes. But the evocative memories went deeper, striking at some sensitive nerve deep inside him. For the first time in his life, Donovan was face to face with something he couldn't analyze. Swamped by desire, overwhelmed by another emotion too staggering to fully understand, he tightened his grip on her silk-clad shoulders.

"While a great many of our nights may have been sleepless, you didn't spend them all worrying, Brooke."

An enervating warmth swept through her body in response to his sensually spoken words. "I really have to leave," she said weakly.

Sometime between the baklava and this moment, Donovan's vast store of patience had run out. Brooke had proven a challenge and he'd always thrived on challenge. But the time had come for him to regain control of the situation.

"You're coming home with me, Brooke. It's time." His jaw firmed. "Hell, it's long past time."

Brooke tried to muster up some lingering flame of resentment and found it to be an impossible task. "You make it sound as if I don't have a choice."

His green eyes were disturbingly intense in the spreading glow of the streetlight. "You don't. Neither of us has had a choice from the beginning, love. If I can see that, even with my admittedly deserved reputation for ignoring life's little subtleties, why can't you?"

Try as she might, Brooke couldn't drag her eyes away from his hypnotizing gaze. "Because I haven't wanted to."

Donovan arched a dark, challenging brow. "And now?"

Brooke breathed a soft sigh of surrender. "As hard as it has been fighting you, Donovan, it's been even more difficult fighting myself."

Donovan fought down the sudden surge of exaltation, afraid that he might have misunderstood. "Does that mean what I think it does?" he asked carefully.

She inclined her head. "I'll go home with you."

He drew her into his arms, giving her a long heartfelt kiss. "You won't be sorry," he promised, resting his chin atop her dark head.

But as Brooke fought back the traitorous tears stinging at her eyelids, she realized that she already was.

Chapter Six

They didn't speak as Donovan drove Brooke's car the few blocks to his house. There was no need. The air practically crackled with the electricity surrounding them.

When she entered the cluttered living room, Brooke couldn't help comparing this with the first time she and Donovan had made love. That night their lovemaking had been a spontaneous thing, unplanned, unavoidable. When she measured it with this evening's calculated sex, Brooke experienced a slight pang of bittersweet regret.

"Would you like a drink?" Donovan asked, seeking something, anything, that would break the nerve-racking silence.

"Nothing for me, thanks." Brooke forced a slight smile. "My head's already spinning."

"There's juice in the fridge."

"Really, I'm fine."

Donovan forced himself to keep his distance. The scene had been set, it was up to Brooke to make the next move. He watched her from across the room.

"You're a lot more than fine, Brooke," he murmured, drinking in that bright, golden fragrance he suddenly realized had haunted him on more than one occasion over the intervening years. Unfortunately he had been too distracted to concentrate on its origin. If he hadn't been, perhaps he could have set things right long ago.

He rubbed the bridge of his nose in a thoughtful gesture Brooke recognized immediately. "Is something wrong?" she asked quietly. For a brief, frightening moment it occurred to her that Donovan might be prepared to forgo their lovemaking.

"I just realized how long I've been waiting for this."

"Since July, wasn't it?"

"Longer." Unable to resist touching her, he crossed the distance between them, lifting her dark hair, sifting it through his fingers. The scent of sunshine clung to its silky strands. "Much, much longer."

Brooke's eyes were veiled by her thick fringe of dark lashes as she looked down at the floor. Putting a finger under her chin, Donovan gently coaxed her gaze to his.

"There's still time to change your mind."

Entranced by the storm brewing in his green eyes, Brooke pressed her palm against his cheek. She wanted this man. She yearned to experience once more the passion that had been missing for so long from her life.

There would be consequences. There were always consequences. Too much was still unsettled between them. But with an impetuousness she had forgotten she possessed, Brooke refused to consider any possible repercussions. There would be time enough for that tomorrow. Tonight, for just this one enchanted evening, she was going to recapture a love she'd thought she had lost for all time.

"I'm not going to change my mind." As she said the words aloud, Brooke found strength in them. A bridge had been burned. It was time to discover what was waiting for her on the other side.

Despite the resolve in her voice, anxiety lingered in her gaze. But desire was there, as well. And anticipation. Donovan clung to these as he stroked her upper arms in what was meant to be a comforting gesture.

"I won't hurt you, Brooke."

Yes, you will, she answered mentally. *You won't want to, but you will.* Her fingers moved to the silk-covered buttons of her dress.

"Not yet." Donovan took her hands in his, lifting them to his lips where he pressed them against his encouraging smile. "We've all night."

Brooke exhaled a slight gasp of surprise when he lifted her into his arms and carried her into the bedroom. "I don't remember you being so romantic."

He was still smiling as he covered her lips with a fleeting kiss. Brooke's toes curled in her suede pumps. "Age offers a few rewards."

She felt the mattress sink under her weight. A moment later he was lying beside her. "Did I tell you how beautiful you are this evening?" he asked, idly tracing the swirling paisley pattern of her russet and gold silk dress.

Brooke caught her breath as his fingertips grazed her breast. "I don't believe it came up."

His sigh was heavy with regret. "And here I thought I was improving." His hand trailed over her hip, down her thigh. "You are exquisite this evening, Brooke Stirling. Enchanting.'' Donovan punctuated his words with soft, feathery kisses. "Ravishing."

Brooke felt as if his light touch had seared the silk to her flesh. She swallowed. "You don't have to do this," she protested softly.

He lifted a brow as his fingers toyed with her gold belt buckle. "Do what?"

Brooke had to push the words past the lump in her throat. "Seduce me. I've already admitted that I want you to make love to me, Donovan."

"I'm going to make love with you," he corrected. "And for the record, that's what I'm doing." A light of gentle amusement shone in the stormy passion of his eyes. "Fortunately for both of us, I've developed some small modicum of control over the years."

Her belt drifted to the floor as his fingers moved quickly, deftly, on the buttons of her dress. When he viewed the creamy flesh clad in an ivory chemise, Donovan groaned softly.

"Strike that previous statement," he rasped. "My so-called control is rapidly disintegrating."

Brooke twined her arms around his neck to pull his head down to hers. "Show me."

Without warning, the storm that had been gathering in his eyes broke free. Lightning flashed, thunder rumbled threateningly. The roar of the wind sounded in her head as his blazing kiss pulled her into the swirling vortex that had Donovan at the center. Passion exploded, hot and unrestrained.

He pressed his lips against her throat before trailing them down the heated flesh between her breasts. As he inhaled the soft scent of her skin, Donovan thought he'd go out of his mind.

"I need to see you."

Brooke clung to him, unable to do otherwise. "Yes."

He slid the dress off her body. Impatient, Brooke lifted her hips, anxious to rid herself of the confining panty hose. To her vast relief, Donovan complied immediately. When he placed a trail of stinging little kisses up first one leg and then the other, she cried out her pleasure.

"That's right," he said, the heat of his mouth warming her skin through the silky chemise. "Don't hold anything back from me. Not tonight, Brooke. Not when I need you so badly." He pushed aside the creamy lace covering her breasts.

"I need you," Brooke countered on a gasp as Donovan traced a path with his tongue from the base of her breasts to the nipples, then back again.

He was relentless, driving her deeper and deeper into the swirling vortex of passion with his lips, his teeth, his tongue. A myriad of sensations flashed through her—the heat of his mouth, the silky texture of his hair as it brushed over her stomach, the heady, masculine scent emanating from his skin.

She had to touch him. With hands that trembled only slightly, Brooke freed him of his shirt, running her hands over the hard muscle, the softly matted hair. When her fingers trailed down his rib cage, lingering over his stomach, before slipping under the waistband of his slacks, Brooke felt Donovan's indrawn breath.

"My God," he said on a deep groan, "I'd nearly forgotten what it felt like to have your hands on me. Undress me, Brooke. I need to feel your tender touch."

Unable to refuse him anything, she slipped the shirt off his shoulders. Heat. It poured off him in waves. She could feel it. And as she pressed her lips against his chest, Brooke imagined she could taste the warmth. She fumbled a bit as she worked the buckle to his belt and her own escalating desire made her gestures a bit awkward, but soon Donovan was pulling her into his arms, clad only in a pair of low-rise cotton briefs.

He was beautiful. His skin, moist with a fine sheen of perspiration, gleamed like polished teak. His body was lean, hard and fully aroused. Donovan Kincaid was all male. And for this one glorious night, he was hers.

"So lovely," he murmured as he stripped the satiny chemise from her trembling body, his lips warming each little bit of freed skin. His fingers roamed lingeringly from shoulder to thigh, leaving her feeling as if a thousand tiny pulses were beating beneath her skin.

His hands were never still, creating flashes of exquisite lightning everywhere they touched. He tugged at a rosy nipple, and Brooke experienced an answering pull deep inside her body. He trailed his short, square fingernails lightly, almost absently, up the silky skin of her inner thigh and Brooke felt her body stir, then begin to soften in response. When he pressed his palm against her stomach, a warmth flowed outward from her innermost core.

Just when Brooke thought she could take no more of his tender torment, Donovan's lips replaced his hands, moving over her with sensual purpose, tasting the satiny skin his touch had warmed. His lips and tongue made exquisite love to her, stroking, nipping, licking, until she knew she would go mad. The quivering that had begun as a slight tremor now had her writhing underneath him, seeking release.

"Now," she pleaded as his fingers explored the heart of her desire with an enthrallingly intimate touch.

"Not yet." Donovan relentlessly ignored her plea, leading her further and further into the storm.

As he continued to incite Brooke's passion, Donovan found his own rising, as well. And when she decided to take matters into her own hands, stroking and kissing him with a hunger that equaled his own, Donovan realized that the tables had suddenly turned.

It had been his plan to seduce Brooke, to make love to her in such a way that she'd have to admit to the inevitability of their relationship. But with soft murmurs and quiet sighs, with gentle hands and tender lips, she had led him to join her at the very brink of madness.

"Donovan." Her eyes, as they looked up into his, resembled molten gold, hot and gleaming. This time Donovan didn't have the strength to ignore her unspoken request.

"Brooke."

He molded his mouth to hers as they entered the hurricane together. Gripping her hips, he rolled her over on top of him and for one brief blinding moment as they joined, it flashed through his mind that nothing had ever felt so right as this. Then there were no more thoughts.

The storm raged for what seemed an eternity. Lightning flashed through her blood, thunder rumbled in her ears. She and Donovan were captives in a place of blinding power, surrounded by flaming heat and dazzling light. And then the turbulent passion passed, leaving behind a slow, cooling languor.

Brooke lay beside him, her legs entwined with his. Her cheek rested on his chest, her dark hair splayed over his body.

"Incredible," he murmured, pressing his lips against the top of her head.

She kept her eyes closed as she idly played with the soft curls covering his chest. He hadn't had this much body hair in their undergraduate days. Just a light sprinkling down the center of his body. She decided she could stay like this forever.

"Is that a critique?" Brooke pressed her lips against his chest. She could feel his heart slowing to a more normal rhythm.

"Not exactly."

Donovan combed his fingers through her love-tousled hair. He decided he liked the new style. It suited who she was today. The woman she had become. His woman, he thought with a surge of masculine possessiveness he wasn't certain Brooke would appreciate, were she to know his true feelings. Donovan was himself a little startled to discover that he possessed that age-old, admittedly chauvinistic mentality that decreed that once a man had made love to a woman, she was his for all time.

Brooke's eyelids opened lazily and she lifted her head to look up at him. "What, exactly?"

"I was thinking how perfect it all was. How it was as if nothing had changed."

Brooke knew what he meant. But for now, until she had time to sort out her feelings, she didn't want to examine the idea that making love with Donovan had indeed been perfect. It had seemed so very, very right.

"A lot has changed," she argued, raising up on one elbow. "We're not kids any longer, Donovan. We're adults. With our own lives. You have your work and I have mine."

At her words, the golden afterglow of their lovemaking began to disintegrate. "Separate, but equal, is that what you mean?"

Brooke decided to ignore the gritty warning in his tone. "Precisely," she said with a brief nod.

Muttering a short oath, Donovan pulled himself up against the headboard. He folded his arms over his bare chest as he looked down at her. "That's ridiculous."

"What's ridiculous? My having my own career? If I recall, you mentioned something about the need for me to quit living through you when you sent me packing."

Frustrated, he dragged his fingers through his hair. "I never sent you packing."

"You said you wouldn't marry me."

"Then," he argued roughly. "I said that it wouldn't be a good idea for me to marry you *then*."

"So what was I supposed to do?" she asked acidly, anger that she had thought long dormant flaring to the surface. "Follow you to Cornell and continue to sit at your feet like some loyal groupie while you dedicated your life to working with those damn chimps? Was I expected to remain available, just in case you felt the urge to ease your sexual frustrations every so often before rushing back to the lab?"

"Is that how you saw our relationship?" he asked, honestly curious.

In those days, it had never occurred to him that Brooke had resented his work. She'd certainly never brought it up. Not until last week, he remembered. Donovan wondered idly if she had been living with that lingering resentment all these years.

"I suppose it is," she admitted, meeting his questioning gaze with a level one of her own.

"You never said anything."

"I was afraid of losing you."

"I loved you," he pointed out. "Surely you knew that."

Brooke decided to be honest. "You certainly never told me you loved me. Besides, if you really did, in my book love equaled marriage."

"Since when?" he challenged, his own irritation flaring at her coolly stated accusation.

Brooke lifted her bare shoulders in a slight shrug. "Since the beginning, I suppose. It was just the way I was brought up."

Uncomfortable with his sudden, blistering glare, she pulled the sheet up over her breasts. Donovan arched a mocking brow at her display of modesty but chose not to comment on it.

"Well, you sure as hell could have fooled me," he said gruffly. "Perhaps you should have majored in drama instead of finance, sweetheart. Because you spent the two years we were together repeating the same lines everyone else was spouting in those days. Free love. Sex without ties. We were supposed to be the liberated generation, remember?"

Brooke pretended a sudden interest in the blue and brown plaid pattern of the rumpled sheet. "I only said all that because it was what you wanted to hear."

Having spent the summer regretting past mistakes, Donovan could have shaken her until those lovely teeth rattled. During this uncharacteristic period of introspection, he had accused himself of acting harshly, of misreading the depth of Brooke's feelings for him. Now, by her own admission, he realized she hadn't been entirely blameless in the fiasco.

"What I wanted to hear?" he repeated under his breath. His eyes gleamed with emerald fire. "And she has the nerve to accuse me of not taking our relationship seriously," he muttered scathingly.

His long fingers gripped Brooke's bare shoulders as he held her suddenly wary gaze to his. "Do you want to know what I really wanted? Did you ever, for just a single moment, consider my feelings?"

"I knew your feelings," she answered stiffly.

"No." His fingers dug into her flesh. "The hell you did. I wanted you, Brooke. More than any woman I'd ever known. More than I thought possible. I wanted us to spend the rest of our lives together."

His deep voice was husky with old resentments. Stunned, Brooke could only stare up at him, both frightened and intrigued by the renewed storm brewing in his eyes.

"But you were so busy playing the liberated female, I was afraid to say anything. I didn't want to sound old-fashioned. Especially when the only reasons you could cite for marrying me were financial ones."

His mouth twisted. "Then you got that terrific job offer a week before graduation and I was forced to accept the idea that to ask you to chuck it in order to live with some impoverished grad student smacked of male chauvinism. Lord knows, in those days, no self-respecting, enlightened young man would have wanted to be accused of that cardinal sin. Besides, to ask you to make such a sacrifice, after the life-style you were accustomed to, would have been excessively selfish, even for me."

Donovan's gaze softened slightly and he managed a ghost of a smile. "I think we've both agreed that I was admittedly a little self-centered in my younger years."

Yesterday, Brooke would have agreed wholeheartedly with that statement. Even earlier this evening she would have professed Donovan Kincaid to have been the most egocentric man she had ever known. Now, however, Brooke was forced to realize that her perceptions of him had been filtered through her own charade of what she had thought he wanted in a woman.

She shook her head, wondering if they would ever be able to sort out the misconceptions on both sides. And even if they could, what would be the point? Brooke felt a sudden need to change the subject.

"Would you do me a favor?" she asked softly, her fingers tracing a royal blue square on the sheet.

"Anything," he answered without hesitation.

She looked up at him, her eyes gleaming through a veil of lush, dark lashes. "Would you kiss me again? No one has ever kissed me the way you do, Donovan."

Groaning his acceptance, Donovan drew her into his arms. He had never thought of himself as a greedy man; his needs had always been simple. A roof over his head, a meal in his stomach, his work, and from time to time a willing woman to warm his bed. But he was beginning to realize that he would never have enough of Brooke.

One touch of her silken skin left his fingers aching for more. One taste and he found himself possessed of a hunger that only she could satisfy. Donovan now knew what it felt like to be sinking into quicksand and, God help him, if the alternative was a life without Brooke, he didn't want to be rescued.

"So much for self-control," he muttered, pressing her deep into the mattress, flesh against flesh.

"You're getting what?" Serena Bedare, nee Lawrence, asked incredulously the following day. She stopped shredding the lettuce to stare across the kitchen at her brother.

"Married. Want me to open the wine? I bought some champagne to celebrate, but upon further consideration I decided it would be better to save that until the wedding.'' Donovan held up the bottle for her perusal. ''This should be good, though, don't you think?''

''I'm sure it's fine,'' Serena murmured, paying no attention whatsoever to the wine as she continued looking up at an amazingly composed, considering the circumstances, Donovan. ''How many bottles of that stuff have you already consumed today?'' she asked suspiciously.

''I haven't so much as sniffed a cork.'' Donovan took up the dinner preparations where Serena left off, tearing the lettuce into bite-size pieces. ''So when's Alex getting home from his symposium? I'm starving.''

''He told me they usually finish up early the first day,'' she said, glancing up at the copper kitchen wall clock. ''He should be home any time now.''

''I'll start the charcoal,'' Donovan offered. ''Where are the steaks?''

''In the supermarket counter, I suppose. We're having hamburgers.'' She began slicing radishes for the salad.

''Serena, when I called you at the club, I explained this was a celebration,'' he complained.

''You also told me not to fuss,'' Serena reminded him. ''Alex and I only got back in town yesterday and practice ran late this afternoon, Donovan. I didn't have time to go to the store.''

Donovan experienced a sharp stab of guilt as he realized that he had been so caught up in his own exciting news that he had forgotten that Serena was working overtime, preparing for the upcoming Australian Open tennis tournament. Having taken two years off to recuperate from injuries sustained in a car accident, the former teenage sweetheart of tennis had staged a remarkable comeback.

After warming up with the Foro Italico in Rome, she had swept the French Open, Wimbledon and, shortly after her marriage to Alex Bedare this past July, the U.S. Open. All she needed now was the Australian to make it a Grand Slam.

As much as Donovan had wanted to spend this evening with Brooke, basking in the idea of their newly found love, she had begged off, claiming a meeting with the various department heads that was expected to run late. He had been somewhat annoyed when she refused his offer to drop by after the meeting, but Donovan reminded himself that while managing a romance with their demanding schedules wasn't going to be easy, nothing worthwhile ever was.

"Want me to run to the store and buy some steaks?" he offered expansively.

"I'd rather you stay here and tell me what's gotten into that rather addlepated head of yours."

"Addlepated?" He flung his hand against his chest. "Is that any way to talk about your brilliant older brother?"

Her gray eyes danced with affection. "Is this the same brother who put my invitation to the White House in the freezer? Along with his gas bill?"

"Guilty," he admitted as he popped a scarlet radish into his mouth. "But as you know, sister dear, I have a very compartmentalized mind. While I am more than capable of conjuring up the author of an obscure fifty-year-old scientific report as quickly as you can snap those talented fingers, I suppose I'd be forced to admit that if you were to ask me what I had for breakfast this morning, you'd be hard-pressed to get an answer."

"Is there a chance that this compartmentalized mind might possibly be capable of coming up with the name of your fiancée?"

"Brooke." Donovan repeated her name, just for the pleasure of savoring it on his tongue. "Brooke Stirling. Isn't that the loveliest name you've ever heard?"

"Simply scrumptious," Serena replied absently as she attempted to place the familiar-sounding name. When she did, the knife stopped its rapid-fire slicing. "This wouldn't be the same Brooke Stirling who let you get away so many years ago, would it? The one whose ancestor is hanging in the foyer of President Chambers's house?"

"Althea D. Smiley," Donovan acknowledged, crunching on a carrot stick. "Feminist, founder and first president of the Althea D. Smiley Coeducational College." He grinned as he quoted the college catalog. "'A bold experiment destined to prove for all time that it is possible for women to share in an Ivy League-styled learning experience without either sex—male or female—suffering substandard education.'

"Good old Althea was Brooke's great-great-aunt." His brow furrowed. "To tell you the truth, I can't remember precisely how many greats. But there were a bunch."

Serena slapped Donovan's hand as he reached for another radish. "With your rather vague memory, I'm surprised you can remember anything about the woman." She gave him her sweetest smile. "Unless, of course, she happens to look like a *Gorilla gorilla beringei*?"

"Who looks like a gorilla?" A deep voice boomed out from the front room, announcing Alex Bedare's arrival.

"Alex," Donovan complained as the tall, dark-haired man entered the kitchen, his lips curved in greeting under his dark mustache, "I thought all you sheikhs taught your women obedience."

"Serena's incorrigible," he answered easily as he wrapped his arms around his wife and gave her a long, welcoming kiss.

Despite the fact that he and Serena had been married for two glorious months, Alex could not get over the sense of wonderment he experienced every time he came home to her loving arms. He doubted that he ever would.

"You should beat her," Donovan decided.

"I tried that," Alex said after they had finally come up for air.

"Well, it obviously didn't take. You must have done something wrong."

"Serena's a very liberated lady—she insisted on beating me back." His midnight eyes laughed down into his wife's as they shared a smile. "Your sister, Donovan, my friend, has a wicked backhand."

"She still shouldn't accuse my bride-to-be of looking like a gorilla," Donovan protested.

"Bride-to-be?" Alex gave Serena a questioning look. She offered a bemused shrug in return.

"I'm getting married," Donovan announced solemnly.

"Congratulations," Alex said promptly. "It's a marvelous state. As far as I'm convinced, everyone should be married. Who's the lucky lady?"

"Brooke Stirling," Serena told him.

Alex arched a dark brow. "Brooke Stirling? The dragon lady in Appropriations?"

"The dragon in Appropriations is Mrs. Harrigan, Brooke's iron lady secretary," Donovan corrected firmly. "Brooke is an absolute angel."

"That's not the scuttlebutt I've been hearing," Alex insisted. "The word is that she's slashing everyone's budget with a hacksaw."

Donovan was not in the mood to hear a single word against the woman he loved. When he had first kissed Brooke, Donovan had suspected that he still loved her. Their lovemaking had only supplied irrefutable proof of his feelings. That was when he had made the decision to marry her.

"You know how faculty gossip is," Donovan argued. "One disgruntled individual gets a crazy idea into his head and soon what's nothing more than gossip is being repeated from department to department."

Alex shrugged as he poured a glass of wine for himself and one for Donovan. Serena smiled her thanks as he handed her a glass of cranberry juice.

"That may be," Alex agreed. "However, I had lunch with Oscar Stevenson today. He's expecting some unprecedented cuts." He took a tentative sip of the ruby Cabernet Sauvignon. "Hey, this isn't half bad." Alex picked up the bottle to study the label. "Did you actually spend your hard-earned dollars on something besides those overeducated apes?"

"I decided to splurge. After all, it isn't every day a man announces his engagement to his family." Donovan took a drink of his own wine. "As for Stevenson, the guy turns in a want list for his beloved chemistry department every year as long as my arm. He always asks for precisely twice what he really needs; that way, no matter what the fiscal situation, he ends up with more than anyone else." He grinned. "Hell, he was doing that when I was a student here."

"I don't know," Alex mused aloud. "He told me that your fiancée returned his budget request with a memo suggesting that since he had such a talent for creating fiction, perhaps he should consider transferring to the Language and Literature department."

Donovan laughed. "Serves the old guy right for trying to pull the wool over her eyes," he said proudly. "Brooke is one smart cookie. She isn't going to be handing out checks for fraudulent or frivolous claims."

"Speaking of frivolous claims," Serena broke in, "what's the chances of Gloria getting a new television before the one she has now blows up?"

Donovan waved away the veiled warning in her tone. "No sweat," he assured her. "Brooke is bound to understand the importance of my work, Serena. She'll come through. I'm convinced of it."

Alex and Serena exchanged a brief glance. "Donovan, you wouldn't . . ." Serena's voice trailed off.

"Propose to Brooke in order to win my grant money?" he finished for her. "Of course not." His brow furrowed. "It could look that way though, couldn't it?"

"You have to admit," Alex put in, "that your timing is a little less than ideal. After all, up till now you've lived the life of a quintessential bachelor, never getting seriously involved with anything but your work."

"Which you take more than seriously," Serena added. "I believe the word might be obsession."

Alex nodded, confirming Serena's observation. "Then, out of the clear blue sky an old flame returns to the college. A woman who just happens to be in the position to grant you the single most important thing in your life. Funds to continue your research."

"And the first day I meet with her," Donovan continued the story, "I drag her into bed."

"Really?" Serena asked with renewed interest. She closed her mouth determinedly when her husband shot her a warning glance.

"Almost," Donovan amended, sinking down into a chair. He dragged his hands through his hair. "You're right. It doesn't look good. No wonder Brooke accused me of using unfair tactics."

"It is a remarkable sequence of events," Serena said. "I never would have suspected that you'd fall in love so fast, Donovan. I would have guessed that you'd spend the first ten years analyzing your feelings, trying to come up with scientific grounds to propose."

Donovan smiled. "It's as much a surprise to me as it is to both of you. I don't know, perhaps it's a deeply repressed regret for having passed up a golden opportunity so many years ago. Or maybe it's seeing how happy marriage has made you two."

His gaze moved over his sister and brother-in-law. "All I know is that the minute I saw her, I knew that she was going to change my life. By the time we made love, I knew precisely what I wanted."

"You're fortunate Brooke shares your feelings," Serena said.

"She doesn't exactly," Donovan admitted. "But I'm sure she'll be all for the idea. In time." He frowned. "Now that you've pointed out how it looks, perhaps I'd better wait a while to propose."

"Don't do that," Alex and Serena said in unison.

Serena looked questioningly at Alex, who nodded in response. A moment later she left the room.

"Don't make the same mistake I did," Alex advised, suddenly serious. "I kept waiting for the right time to tell

Serena how I felt about her. All that happened was that I managed to send her a lot of false signals, then blurted it out at the worst possible time.'' He refilled Donovan's wineglass. ''You'll save yourself a lot of headaches if you tell the lady at the first opportunity.''

''But be prepared to give her some time,'' Serena warned as she returned to the kitchen. ''After all, not everyone is blessed with your brilliant insight,'' she teased. ''Close your eyes and hold out your hand.''

''Why?''

''Don't argue, Donovan. Just give me your hand.''

As Donovan complied, he felt cold metal against his palm. Opening his eyes, he viewed the worn Lincoln penny.

''It's a lucky penny,'' Serena explained. ''Alex gave it to me before Wimbledon.''

''Thanks a lot, honey, but you know I don't believe in luck.''

''I won Wimbledon,'' she reminded him.

''You're talented.''

''I was also ill. Not to mention the fact that Alex and I broke up right before I had to drag my flu-riddled body onto Centre Court.'' She shook her head, refusing to take back the coin. ''It's lucky, Donovan. I know it is.'' She looked up at her husband beseechingly. ''Tell him, darling.''

''It got me Serena.''

Donovan knew Alex to be an intelligent, broad-minded individual. Before arriving at Smiley a year ago to lecture in International Relations, the man had experienced a brilliant career as a diplomat. Donovan had met Alex Bedare's American mother at the wedding, and she had appeared to be a nice, practical woman who would eschew beliefs in magic charms and spells. Donovan decided that Alex must have inherited this distressing streak of mysticism from his Egyptian father.

"You can't really believe that," he argued, not wanting to discover this fatal flaw in his friend and family member.

"In the beginning I felt the same way you do," Alex assured him. "When Carly Ryan gave me the coin."

"The woman who married your old friend from Oxford?"

Alex nodded. "And the mother of my godson. Carly and Patrick are highly intelligent people. Yet they both swore to me that the penny you're holding in your hand not only brought them together, but helped them survive a tempestuous affair that made Serena's and mine appear uneventfully placid by comparison."

Donovan was having a difficult time believing his ears. "Are you telling me that you're all members of some weird cult? Next you'll be shaving your heads, chanting mantras and selling flowers in airport terminals."

Alex laughed heartily. "Now you're exaggerating. However, whatever you want to believe, Donovan, my friend, if you keep that penny with you at all times, eventually you'll begin to realize that Carly's grandfather was right. It does seem to have some strange, inexplicable power."

Donovan arched a disbelieving brow. "Now we've got a grandfather in the saga of the mystical lucky penny?"

"Laugh all you want, Donovan Kincaid," Serena said. "But Carly's grandfather was a magician. So he should know."

"An illusionist," Donovan corrected. "That's what magicians do, Serena. They create illusions, fooling your mind with tricks of the eye. That's all there is to it."

Her expression was as sober as he'd ever seen it. "Be that as it may," she said quietly, "promise me that you'll keep Carly's lucky penny."

Donovan shook his head. It was ridiculous. He was a man of science. He'd be laughed out of the profession if it became known that he carried a lucky coin around with him.

"Serena, I know you mean well but—"

She closed his fingers around the metal talisman. "Can't you humor your sister? Just for a short time?"

"For how long?" he asked with a sigh, knowing that he would give in, as he always had.

Although they weren't related by blood—his father had married her mother when Donovan was thirteen and Serena was eight—there was no one he loved more dearly.

Serena gave the matter careful thought. "Until Thanksgiving break," she decided.

"Thanksgiving! That's nearly three months from now," he complained.

She reached up to pat his cheek. "From what I can remember, you messed up royally twelve years ago, Donovan, dear. While Carly's lucky penny is magic, miracles take a little more time." She looked over at Alex. "I'd say three months should do it. Wouldn't you, darling?"

"Indubitably," he agreed.

Feeling incredibly foolish, Donovan mustered up an off-center smile in return for the dazzling ones Serena and Alex were bestowing upon him.

Later that night as he undressed for bed, Donovan failed to notice the coin fall onto the floor and roll under the bed. As he lay awake long into the night, staring at the ceiling, his head braced by his folded arms as he contemplated Brooke's return to his life, Donovan put the allegedly lucky penny from his mind.

Chapter Seven

So much for scientific method, Donovan told himself
two weeks later. He threw down his pen, giving up on his
work for the time being. It was more than a little disconcerting to discover that the laws by which he had
lived his life were of no help in his relationship with
Brooke.

If observed facts were the foundation of the scientific
method and ultimately the proof of its results, then
Donovan knew he was on firm ground. It did not take a
very keen sense of observation to determine that Brooke
was not immune to him; her lovemaking had proven
that. Still, what they had shared was more than sex. It
was a merging of mind and body, a mingling of souls,
something as mystical as it was physical. All this he had
observed. And more.

Point two: scientific observation must be repeated at
will. On this point, also, Donovan was in safe territory.
As if feeling the need to make up for lost years, he and
Brooke had made love innumerable times during the past

two weeks, leaving Donovan stunned by his greed, his insatiable hunger for her.

Point three: the facts derived from repeated observation must be clear to anyone. Neither he nor Brooke had made any overt attempt to hide their relationship, but neither did they flaunt it. Nevertheless he couldn't help noticing that Brooke's guardian dragon, Mrs. Harrigan, had actually offered him a dry, accepting smile when he had shown up at her office yesterday afternoon. Stephanie had brought up her name on more than one occasion.

Even Gloria had asked repeatedly when Brooke was going to visit again. Of course, Donovan admitted, rising from the desk to stare out the window, the gorilla's primary interest appeared to be a new television set.

A young couple stopped to share a lingering kiss under the shade of a spreading oak tree, reminding Donovan that it had been too long since he'd last kissed Brooke. Desire flared, strong and unrelenting, and he glanced down at his watch, counting the hours until he could be alone with her. In an attempt to restrain his building hunger, Donovan forced his thoughts back to his initial problem.

About the observations themselves, there could be no dispute. He felt extremely comfortable with this part of the equation; the insistence on accurate observational data was one of the great virtues of scientific reasoning.

But when it came to predicting results, to formulating a hypothesis, his method failed miserably. The scientific foundation of his study crumbled like a sand castle at high tide. Donovan had predicted that, like himself, Brooke would welcome the opportunity to set things straight. To correct past misunderstandings. He loved her. And as far as he was concerned, once that love had been realized and shared, marriage was the next logical step. Apparently Brooke disagreed.

During their lovemaking she would be more responsive than any man could imagine. Or dare to hope for. But after passions had cooled, she would revert back to that calm, collected individual that she appeared to have become. What type of woman could be aflame in his arms one moment, then turn practical, unemotional, the next?

"Damn her," he muttered, frowning out at the gray clouds building up on the western horizon.

Despite Alex's and Serena's words of caution, Donovan had been waiting for Brooke to indicate that she, too, wanted a more permanent relationship. When she failed to mention the subject, Donovan held his own tongue, keeping his fantasies to himself. She was quite literally driving him crazy. Donovan wasn't accustomed to anyone, least of all a woman, interfering with his thoughts, his work. He wasn't prepared for such an occurrence and he damn well didn't like it.

What he liked even less was the fact that his heretofore revered scientific reasoning had developed a major flaw. Against his will, Donovan was forced to accept the unpleasant idea that because human values were by nature subjective, the products of an individual's emotions—in this case, Brooke Stirling's—they were therefore impossible to deal with in an objective, quantitative fashion.

For the first time in his life, Donovan felt hopelessly adrift, as if he'd been cast onto a dark, uncharted sea and forced to navigate on instinct alone.

Unaware of Donovan's struggle to understand his obsession with something other than his work, Brooke was having problems of her own. Professor Stevenson's second proposal had proven to be every bit as fanciful as his first. She had no alternative but to go through the items with him, line by line.

"You're asking for a great many flasks, Professor Stevenson," she noted. "Surely it isn't necessary to replace your entire inventory each semester."

The man's sparse gray mustache twitched above thin lips. "Breakage."

"We must have a great many careless students." Brooke didn't bother to disguise the irony in her tone.

His eyes, through the thick lenses of his wire-framed trifocals, remained implacable. "You know kids nowadays. They seem to get clumsier every year."

Brooke tapped her pencil irritably on her yellow notepad as she continued to peruse the man's wish list. She had been instructed to handle the tenured professor with kid gloves. Still, it was also her responsibility to cut costs wherever possible and from what she had been able to tell, Oscar Stevenson was a prime candidate for the budget ax.

"Yes. Well, be that as it may, I'm having a difficult time believing that so many of our chemistry students can't hang on to a simple glass beaker." Brooke gave him an innocent smile. "Perhaps it's more a case of being light-fingered," she suggested sweetly.

He scowled. "What the blue blazes does that mean?"

Brooke put her pencil down and folded her hands on her desktop. "Come on, Dr. Stevenson," she protested on a weary sigh, "we're not going to get anywhere beating around the bush like this. You're requesting an unreasonable amount of beakers and flasks. Also several new burners and an extraordinary amount of tubing. What would you say if I suggested that some of our more industrious students were indulging in a little extracurricular entrepreneurship?''

The elderly man bristled. His scalp, visible through his thin pewter hair, flushed crimson. "Are you daring to suggest that those supplies are being stolen by Smiley College students in order to distill illegal liquor?''

She gave him a rewarding smile. "That's precisely what I'm suggesting, Professor. You may be interested in knowing that your recent rash of *breakage* coincides perfectly with the mysterious disappearance of several bushels of potatoes from the dining hall kitchens.''

When he appeared absolutely thunderstruck, Brooke mentally gave the man points for his outraged performance. "Well, I for one refuse to believe such accusations,'' he argued. "After all, many of our students come from the highest echelons of society. They are accustomed to the best our capitalistic system has to offer. Why should they stoop to make bootleg alcohol?''

"Tradition, Professor,'' she replied smoothly. "Now, if we channel the money routinely spent on additional supplies to improved locks for the chemistry labs, I believe we can slow down your dwindling inventory.''

Brooke ignored the professor's frustrated huffing and puffing as she scribbled a brief notation in the margin.

"Now,'' she said slowly, carefully, folding her hands again and leaning toward him, "as to the request for uranium—''

"U235,'' he interjected helpfully.

Brooke nodded. "That's right. I'm afraid that your request is totally out of the question, Doctor.''

"I certainly don't see why you'd feel that way.''

"Don't you?'' she challenged quietly.

"It's important that our students understand the world around them. Nuclear energy is going to be with us, no matter what naysayers and political liberals such as yourself have to say about it," he protested, getting onto a verbal soapbox.

"Whether I am or am not a fan of nuclear energy is not the topic under discussion," Brooke argued. "What you're suggesting, Dr. Stevenson, is quite probably illegal. Not to mention downright dangerous."

"Only for those ill prepared to handle the substance," he countered. "Since I don't recall having you in any of my classes, Miss Stirling, let me give you a few basic facts regarding the atom."

"Go ahead," Brooke agreed, ignoring his sarcastic swipe at what he obviously considered an enormous gap in her education. She was prepared to humor the man. To a point.

"If precisely one neutron per fission causes another fission, energy will be released at a constant rate. This is the case in a nuclear reactor; it is this demonstration I wish my students to experience."

Brooke was glad that she'd taken the time to do her homework. She leaned back in her chair and crossed her legs. "Even if I were to approve funding for a nuclear reactor, which I most assuredly won't—" she warned, raising her hand to forestall his planned interruption "—the fact remains that if the frequency of fission increases, with more than one neutron from each fission leading to others, the energy release will be so rapid that an explosion will occur."

Her lips firmed as she met his angry gaze. "Unless I'm mistaken, Dr. Stevenson, we are now talking about an atomic bomb."

He was on his feet, a muscle in his jaw twitching as he glared through the thick lenses at her. "And you're sounding precisely like the Church when they declared

Galileo a heretic for his advocacy of the Copernican system. Did you know that the man actually lost his professorship at Pisa for challenging prevailing theories of his time?"

"And are you willing to give up your professorship, Dr. Stevenson?" she asked calmly. "Because that's precisely what will happen if you don't drop this ludicrous idea of nuclear fission in the classroom."

"You, Miss Stirling," he accused through clenched teeth as he jabbed his finger in her direction, "and shortsighted individuals like you will eventually be held responsible for America's dwindling position as democratic armament supplier to the world!"

With that the irate professor stormed out of her office. "Good luck," he warned Donovan, who had inadvertently chosen this unfortunate moment to arrive, "you'll need it with Bloody Brooke at the helm."

"Bloody Brooke, I presume?" Donovan greeted her with a broad grin.

Brooke rubbed her fingers wearily against her temples where she felt the impending twinges of a headache. "Why do I feel as if I've just undergone a debate with Dr. Strangelove?"

"Because you have," Donovan said easily as he came around the desk and took over the chore. "Are his classes still distilling that rotgut vodka?"

"That feels good," Brooke acknowledged as his fingers soothed away her tension. "Of course they are. However, you're a fine one to criticize the man on that score, Donovan Kincaid. If I remember correctly, you ran a thriving little distillery yourself."

"Hey, it's not easy putting yourself through college," he complained. "I had to latch onto every opportunity that presented itself."

"Well, if you have any of those flasks hanging around your house, do Professor Stevenson a favor and drop them by the lab. His budget is right out of fantasyland. I'm going to have to slice it to the bone."

"So I've heard."

She glanced up at him curiously. "People are still talking about me, aren't they?"

Donovan shrugged as he lightly traced her ear with the tip of his finger. "Can you blame them? Face it, love, there's an old saying—'don't cut him and don't cut me, cut that guy behind the tree.' You've got to expect people to feel protective of their own projects."

"Are you?" she couldn't help asking. She had been surprised, but admittedly relieved, when Donovan had not broached the subject of his own research funding the past two weeks.

He dropped his hands, depriving her of the pleasure of his touch. "Hell, yes."

"But you haven't asked me about it. Not since..." Her voice drifted off as soft color flooded into her cheeks.

"Since we made love that first night," he finished for her. He bent down, brushing his lips against hers with a tantalizing touch. "Perhaps I simply decided to try another approach."

A cloud moved across her eyes at the same time an icy hand gripped her heart. "You are kidding, aren't you?"

Donovan stood up and folded his arms over his chest. "What do you think?"

Brooke gave him a killing look. "I think," she said slowly, "that you're a rat even to joke about a horrible thing like that."

Donovan's smile could have melted stone. "And you're beautiful when you're angry."

She tossed her head, repressing her own answering smile. "If you intend to seduce me into approving your budget request, Professor Kincaid, you're going to have to do a lot better than that old cliché."

His green eyes sparkled. "Come home with me and I'll give it the old college try."

As he ran his hand down her arm, Brooke was tempted to do exactly that. The idea that she was forgetting something important teased at the back of her mind, disallowing her to immediately succumb to his provocative invitation.

"The party," she said on a gasp as he bent his head to nibble at her earlobe. "We're both expected at President Chambers's house at seven-thirty."

Damn. He had forgotten all about the annual party to introduce new faculty members. Donovan glanced down at his watch. "We have an hour." He began kissing her neck. "Not as much as I'd like, but enough to give you a sampling of what the night holds in store."

As Donovan's lips trailed down her throat, Brooke could feel her bones literally melting. "Don't do that," she protested, "Mrs. Harrigan is just outside the door. She could come in at any time."

"Uh-uh." He perched on the edge of her desk and began to slowly unbutton her cobalt blouse. "I sent the gorgon home for the day. I also locked the door when I came in."

Brooke frowned. "I didn't notice that."

He flexed his fingers. "Quick hands. Did I mention that my sister is married to a former diplomat?" he inquired as he trailed his index finger along the scalloped lace bodice of her slip.

Brooke was grateful she was sitting down; her legs would never support her. "I believe you mentioned it at dinner the other night," she managed to answer even as his touch was driving her mad. "Why?"

He pushed the midnight-blue lace aside, cupping her breast in his palm. "Alex has friends in high places. I think I'll ask him to get a law passed that prohibits you from covering up these delightful lacy things."

"Good idea. I'd be sure to be a hit walking around campus in my underwear."

"When we're alone," Donovan amended. Brooke drew in a sharp breath as his thumbs flicked casually over her hard nipples. "You'll meet Alex tonight, by the way. He and Serena will be at the party."

Unable to resist the slight parting of her lips as his fingers plucked at the pink crest of her breast, he leaned forward, kissing her with unmistakable purpose.

"Speaking of the party," he said on a deep, regretful sigh once he had released her, "I suppose you're going to insist that we attend."

She brushed an errant lock of crisp brown hair off his forehead. "Since the purpose of the party is to introduce new faculty members to the rest of the college community, I don't have a choice. You're welcome to do what you want, Donovan, but I wouldn't think a little last-minute social lobbying for your funding would do any harm."

Donovan buried his face in the softness of her breasts, drinking in the alluring scent that clung to her skin. He had never been one to romanticize things, but he didn't think he would ever be able to wake up to sunshine again without wanting to make love to Brooke.

"So what do you think I'm doing?" he murmured.

As Brooke's mouth went suddenly dry, she grabbed hold of his hair and tugged. Hard.

"Ow! That hurts, Brooke."

"I told you not to joke about our situation."

He rubbed his head. "So you did. I guess I hadn't realized that you were so serious."

"I am." Her grave eyes echoed her words.

Donovan sighed. "So I see."

He leaned forward, rebuttoning her blouse with obvious regret. She was trembling, not from passion, and it was his fault. Donovan damned his incautious tongue.

"I'm sorry for upsetting you, Brooke. I wouldn't knowingly do that for the world." He took her hand and lifted it to his lips.

Distracted by the feathery caress, Brooke struggled to collect her thoughts. "I accept your apology, Donovan. Just don't do it again."

"I wouldn't think of it." He kissed her fingers, one at a time. "You know, if you didn't have such a damn good memory, we'd be making love right now. Instead of getting ready for another boring faculty party."

"It's my first one," Brooke protested. "I really don't want to miss it."

"They're not that different from the ones you're accustomed to in the corporate arena, Brooke. Nonstop lobbying, with just enough slap and tickle going on in the kitchen to make things interesting."

"You've just piqued my interest. I wonder if that sexy Dr. Williams from the poly sci department is invited?"

Donovan experienced a flash of something he recognized as jealousy. "Don't even think about it," he warned. "Or you'll find yourself in hotter water than you ever thought possible."

Temper flared in her eyes. "You don't have any right to talk to me that way."

"Don't I?"

Heart hammering in her throat, Brooke forced herself to meet his suddenly dangerous gaze. "No, you don't. Now, if you'd let go of my arm, I'd like to go home and change my clothes. Then I'm going to the party. Alone," she tacked on deliberately.

"Don't be an idiot. We're going to that party together, where we'll listen to boring, lengthy anecdotes about everyone's summer vacation."

He ran his hands down her sides, encouraging her to soften her tense stance. "And after we've done our professional duty, I'm taking you home and making slow, passionate love with you all night long."

Brooke didn't resist as Donovan drew her into his arms. "Pretty sure of yourself, aren't you, Professor Kincaid?"

His slow smile touched every portion of his tanned face. "Pretty sure of us." A moment later his mouth captured hers in a kiss that took her breath away.

The party had spilled out onto the lawn. Perfumes—floral, spicy, Oriental, all as individual as the women who wore them—mingled with blue clouds of tobacco smoke and the tangy scent of gold and russet chrysanthemums making up the autumnal garden. Along with the festivity in the air came a sense of renewal. Greetings were exchanged as people caught up on the campus gossip—who had achieved tenure, who had published during the summer hiatus, and even more interesting to most of the partygoers, what prominent, internationally celebrated government lecturer had run off with what lesser acclaimed professor's wife.

Resolutions were made, some of which would inevitably be broken by morning, as they had been last year and the year before that. Other vows would fare better, lasting a week, a month, a selected few even longer. It could have been New Year's Eve; all that was missing were noisemakers, handfuls of colorful confetti to toss at midnight and a dance band to play a stirring rendition of "Auld Lang Syne."

In this community of scholars, unlike in the rest of the world, the new year did not arrive when the calendar turned to January. It began, as it had for the last one hundred years, on the first Tuesday after Labor Day. The first day of classes, the opening day of the fall semester. A time when both students and professors maintained the loftiest of ideals and no goal, no matter how ambitious, seemed out of reach.

"Well," Serena demanded, glancing around the crowded backyard of the college president's large white Georgian manor house, "where is this paragon of femininity?"

Donovan shook his head as he grinned down at her. "I recall a time, my darling sister, when you were much less likely to speak your mind. It's obvious that your husband has been a bad influence on you."

While it was true that she had become more outgoing since Alex had encouraged her to open herself up to all life had to offer, Serena refused to accept Donovan's smiling accusation.

"Pooh," she argued, "you can't expect me not to be curious about the woman you plan on marrying."

"About that—" Donovan began, wanting to warn Serena not to mention the subject to Brooke.

But he wasn't to be given the opportunity. A moment later a familiar fragrance captured his attention and he turned toward the woman who'd come up behind him. The smile on his lips was echoed in the warmth of his eyes.

"I missed you."

Brooke returned his smile with a dry one of her own. "I was invited into President Chambers's private office in order to explain why I had threatened to single-handedly close down the chemistry department. I suppose I shouldn't be surprised that Professor Stevenson went to see him the moment he left my office."

She glanced past him at the waiting couple, recognizing Donovan's sister immediately. Serena Lawrence's face had appeared on magazine covers from the time she was fifteen.

"Since Donovan's obviously forgotten his manners, I suppose it's up to us to introduce ourselves. Hello, I'm Brooke Stirling."

"Of course you are," Serena said, taking the hand Brooke extended. "Donovan described you perfectly. I'm Serena Bedare. And this is my husband, Alex."

"I'm pleased to meet you both," Brooke said with a smile. "Although I don't think I'll dare ask what Donovan has said about me."

Alex's dark eyes gleamed with good-natured humor. "Only that you were the most intelligent, beautiful woman he's ever met."

"And even more enthralling than Gloria," Serena put in, "which was when we realized that he was definitely marrying the right woman. Anyone capable of taking my brother's mind off that talking gorilla has to have something going for her."

Serena's gray eyes narrowed as Brooke suddenly paled. "Uh-oh," she murmured, casting an apologetic glance Donovan's way. "I think I just blew it."

With a calm he was far from feeling, Donovan slipped his arm reassuringly around Brooke's waist. She tensed at the light touch, reminding him of a skittish doe.

"Let's just say that an announcement of matrimony may be a bit premature," he said easily as he returned Serena's distressed look with an understanding smile.

His sister's untimely slip of the tongue was, after all, all his fault; he hadn't told Serena not to mention marriage. Convinced that he and Brooke still belonged together, Donovan hadn't expected Brooke to put up any resistance to making their affair permanent. It was still coming as an unpleasant surprise that she was insisting on setting her own rules this time.

Brooke struggled to keep from revealing exactly how unsettling Serena's teasing words had been. "Don't worry about a thing," she assured Donovan's sister. "Obviously the gossip mongers have been working overtime where Donovan and I are concerned." She managed a shaky laugh. "You know how it is, you have a few lunches with someone and pretty soon the rest of the world has you engaged."

Serena's gaze was sympathetic as she inclined her head ever so slightly. "I know the feeling all too well. That's all the more reason for me not to have blurted it out that way. Believe me, I usually have far better manners."

"Don't worry about a thing," Brooke repeated. "You certainly didn't mean any harm, after all."

Serena didn't know who she felt sorrier for at this moment, her brother or the obviously distraught woman standing beside him. It hadn't been so long ago that she and Alex had been in the throes of their own tumultuous romance. As her husband's hand squeezed hers encouragingly, Serena experienced a vast sense of relief that those problems were well behind them.

"So, Brooke," she said with a bright, encouraging smile, "what do you think of Smiley College so far?"

"I love it. But of course I'm prejudiced."

"It was a relative of yours who established the charter in the first place, wasn't it?" Alex inquired.

Brooke gave him a grateful smile, acknowledging the way he had deftly nudged the conversation in a different direction. "Althea D. Smiley was my great-great-great-aunt. Aunt Althea was an ardent feminist who wanted to prove that women could receive the same education as men, in the same setting, without the quality of instruction suffering for either sex."

"She obviously proved her point," Donovan said, "because Brooke is one of the smartest women I know."

"And she's still willing to put up with you," Serena marveled, patting her brother's cheek affectionately. "How amazing." She grinned at Brooke. "By the way, I appreciate what you've done for my brother's appearance."

"His appearance?"

Serena nodded firmly. "Every time I've managed to catch sight of him lately, he's been wearing matching shoes. And socks."

Three pairs of eyes moved from the top of Donovan's head down to his feet. "It's not that unusual," he complained with a slightly sheepish smile.

"Of course it isn't," Brooke agreed easily, beginning to enjoy the comfortable family banter. Growing up an only child, surrounded by servants, Brooke's conversations at home had always been lacking in the light teasing that seemed to come so easily to Serena and her brother.

She grinned up at Donovan. "The shoes you first put on to wear with that navy suit this evening definitely matched. The fact that they were your running shoes hardly mattered at all."

"Come on, Donovan," Alex said, looping a friendly arm around his brother-in-law's shoulder, "if these sharp-tongued women are going to gang up on you, we may as well go find something to drink."

As the two men walked away, Brooke and Serena exchanged an indulgent look. "You're a lucky woman," Brooke said, her gaze shifting momentarily to Alex Bedare.

Serena's own gray eyes drifted toward her husband and she nodded. "I am, indeed," she agreed on a soft sigh. "Sometimes I think back on all the time I wasted resisting what Alex had to offer and wonder how a clever woman such as myself could have been so foolish."

Brooke thought she could detect a hint of advice in Serena's casual tone. "I watched your Wimbledon final on television," she said, changing the subject. "Both days. It was incredible."

Serena groaned good-naturedly. "The incredible thing was my luck. If the match hadn't been rained out after that first disastrous set, I never could have come back to win."

"The commentators said you were ill."

Serena grimaced. "Sick as a dog," she agreed. "Flu. Of course, the fact that Alex and I had a knock-down-drag-out fight that morning didn't help matters any."

"You two actually fight?" Brooke couldn't help being surprised.

For as long as she could remember, Serena Lawrence had been known as the Ice Princess of the tennis world. The idea that the princess and her debonair, diplomat husband suffered the same petty emotions as the rest of the world came as a revelation.

"It was terrible," Serena divulged. "I didn't know which made me more miserable—that damn flu, or the fact that Alex had just walked out on me."

A cloud moved momentarily across Serena's face, leading Brooke to believe that the memory was still more than a little painful. Realizing that she had allowed her mind to wander, Serena gave a light self-conscious laugh.

"Fortunately he had the good sense to return later that same afternoon. And I was lucky enough to be given another chance at both the match and our relationship."

Serena's expression sobered as she placed a slender hand on Brooke's arm. "I love Donovan," she said seriously. "Next to Alex, there's no one in the world I care about as much as my brother. But I want you to know, Brooke, that if you ever want to talk—woman to woman—I won't let my feelings stand in our way."

Brooke was extremely moved by Serena's words. "Thank you. I appreciate your offer."

The other woman lifted her silk-clad shoulders in a graceful shrug. "Donovan's not easy to live with," she admitted. "He's absentminded—remind me someday to tell you about the time he misplaced my invitation to the White House. And when he's engrossed in his work, the rest of the world could cease to exist for all he cares." She gave Brooke a particularly sagacious look. "But I suspect you already know that."

Brooke nodded. "I learned that lesson years ago."

"Of course you did. You also undoubtedly learned that he doesn't give a fig for parties like this, but he goes to them because he can't pass up an opportunity to hustle up some funds for his research projects. However, he'd close up shop before he'd ever stoop to toadying to

potential benefactors, and if you do agree to marry my
brother, you'll spend a great deal of your precious time
smoothing over his diplomatic lapses.

"But," Serena added with a smile, "you'd also be
getting a man who would stand by you come hell or high
water and who, even if he forgot to tell you as often as
he probably should, would love you more than you ever
believed possible. And from where I sit," Serena said,
her gaze softening as she saw her husband approaching,
"you could do a lot worse."

With that closing advice, she dragged Alex off to meet
a visiting guest lecturer from the English department,
leaving Donovan and Brooke alone for the first time
since arriving at the cocktail party.

"Your sister is nice," Brooke said, accepting the glass
of champagne Donovan handed her.

"I've always thought so. I suppose I should point out
that she's technically my stepsister. Her mother married
my dad when she was eight and I was thirteen."

He took a drink of the aged Scotch. As far as Donovan could tell, President Chambers's admittedly superior brand of liquor was the only thing that made these
faculty affairs reasonably palatable. That and the opportunity to shore up support for his work, of course.

"Unfortunately," he continued, "the marriage didn't
last and I didn't see much of Serena for a time, but we've
always been close, regardless of geography."

"I could tell that," Brooke said thoughtfully. "No
one would ever know that you weren't related by blood."

Donovan shrugged. "We never bothered to make the
distinction. It didn't seem to make a difference."

Brooke's gaze shifted from Donovan across the room
to Alex Bedare. He was gazing down at his wife, his ebony eyes filled with ill-disguised wonder. Serena, en-

gaged in an obviously stimulating conversation with a tall, thin, bespectacled man sporting an unnaturally red toupee, remained oblivious to her husband's loving study.

"Alex certainly seems nice. And he obviously adores Serena."

"Worships the ground she walks on," Donovan agreed. "Fortunately for the balance of power in that relationship, the feeling is mutual." His green eyes roamed over her face. "How long do we have to hang around here?"

The desire in his heated gaze went straight to her heart, causing it to hammer wildly against her ribs. Brooke pressed her hand against the bodice of her black cocktail dress in an unconscious gesture to steady it.

"I suppose that we've done our duty," she said in a voice that was already husky, an intriguing mixture of smoke and honey.

Donovan plucked her glass from her hand, discarding it with his own on a tray carried by a passing waiter. Then, his fingers splayed on her waist, he turned her toward the gate at the other side of the yard.

"Let me be the first to congratulate you on making a very wise and prudent decision."

Brooke looked up at him curiously. "Prudent?"

"Prudent." Leaning down, he caught the lobe of her ear between his teeth. "Because one more minute and I'd be forced to rip that proper little dress off your luscious body, throw you down onto President and Mrs. Chambers's pristinely manicured lawn and make mad, passionate love to you right in front of the entire Althea D. Smiley Coeducational College faculty."

Brooke was amazed by the way her body reacted instinctively, warming to his words. But she didn't challenge Donovan's outrageous statement. The way she was feeling right now, she'd probably take him up on it.

"One thing certainly hasn't changed—you're still incorrigible," she cómplained lightly. His fingers were warming her skin through the silk fabric of her dress as he shepherded her through the crush of people.

Donovan had watched Brooke's eyes widen in response to his words and found himself even more aroused by her reaction. "And aren't you glad I am?"

Tilting her head, Brooke shared a slow, secret smile with him. "Very."

Chapter Eight

Had it been minutes? Or hours? Brooke blinked sleepily as she glanced around the darkened room. Propping herself up on her elbows, she tried to focus on the digital dial of Donovan's clock radio.

"Going somewhere?" Donovan's arm tightened, drawing her back against his warm, inviting body.

"I just changed my mind," she murmured, snuggling down beside him.

"Too bad."

She looked up at him. "You want me to leave?"

He pressed a light kiss against her frowning lips. "Of course not. I thought perhaps you'd been struck by a bolt of domesticity and decided to go into the kitchen and find your man something to eat."

Brooke was feeling lazily satiated and had no desire to go mucking around a kitchen. Especially one as sparsely supplied as Donovan's. The most she'd probably find in his refrigerator would be a stash of fruit that the apes had rejected because it had gone too soft for their finicky tastes.

"You should have eaten at the party. There was enough food there to feed an army."

"My body can only concentrate on one thing at a time," he objected. "After the way you led me on in your office, all I could think about was dragging you back here and having my wicked way with you."

Brooke was unreasonably pleased that she could cause Donovan such physical and mental discomfort. Slowly, almost absently, she ran the bottom of her foot up his calf.

"Well, it's too bad you didn't at least try the butterfly shrimp; they were delicious. I'll admit to being relieved when I discovered that Mrs. Chambers had hired outside caterers. I wasn't particularly looking forward to dining hall fare."

When she pressed her lips against his chest, Donovan's body stirred in automatic response. "You keep that up, sweetheart, and I may just forget that I'm starving to death."

He pulled her on top of him. "Besides, now that you mention it, what's the matter with the dining hall meals? Or do you have something against meat loaf?"

Brooke grinned into his smiling eyes. "Not the first day. Nor do I particularly object to an encore performance for the second night's dinner. But when the stuff showed up cold in the breakfast hash the third morning, I felt the cook was overdoing a good thing."

He ran his hands down the length of her back, his fingers skimming over her hips. "Are you sure you're not hungry?" he asked hopefully.

Brooke nuzzled against him. "Nope."

"I am." Donovan's stomach growled, reinforcing his words.

Exhaling a sigh, Brooke rolled off him. "You're a big boy now, Donovan. So go find yourself something to eat."

He trailed one finger down her cheek. "I was hoping you'd consider it a romantic notion to feed your lover." Devils danced in his gleaming green eyes. "Especially considering all the energy he's expended this evening."

Brooke arched a quizzical brow as she sat up, propping the pillows up behind her as she leaned back against the headboard. "I hadn't realized lovemaking was a solo event. Are you saying that I don't satisfy you, Donovan?"

"Of course not," he hurried to reassure her. "You were wonderful. Stupendous. Incredible, as always."

Brooke fought the smile teasing at the corners of her lips. "But you're still hungry."

"Starving."

She forced a careless shrug. "It's your kitchen, Donovan, not mine." Folding her arms over her breasts, she eyed him somewhat censoriously. "And now that the subject has come up, I'd like to know why we always make love here."

Confused by her suddenly serious tone, Donovan sat up as well. "I thought you liked my house," he complained.

"Of course I do. At least what I can see of it through the clutter. But my apartment isn't exactly a dump, Donovan. Why don't we ever make love there?"

"Because it makes me nervous," he admitted, feeling foolish the moment the words had left his mouth.

"Nervous?"

Donovan shrugged. "Honey, you have a great many wonderful attributes, but if I were forced to name a flaw, it would be that you're an obsessive neatnik. That minimalist apartment of yours reminds me of a nun's cell. Or someplace a surgeon might live. Or an accountant.''

"I *am* an accountant," Brooke pointed out. "And if it's really too neat for your taste, we can always throw a few magazines onto the couch." She smiled encouragingly. "In fact, if it'll make you more comfortable, Donovan, let's go all out. We'll take all the copies of the Encyclopedia Britannica and pile them over the carpeting in varying size pyramids."

She was laughing at him. Donovan wasn't certain he liked that. "Or we could simply keep things the way they are," he grumbled. "What's wrong with making love here?"

"I'm tired of having to go home and change every morning."

"So bring some clothes over," Donovan countered with a casualness he was far from feeling. "Hell, why don't you just move in? You spend all your free time here, anyway."

Brooke stared at him. "Move in here? With you?"

He leaned toward her, his lips inches from hers. "Why not? It seems to me to be the ideal situation."

Her fingers plucked nervously at the sheets. "People will talk."

"I don't care."

Brooke hated admitting that she did. But early socialization ran deep. "Besides, if we lived together," she said tentatively, "couldn't it be argued that we were condoning identical behavior from the students? Encouraging it, even?"

He shot her a frustrated, impatient look. "Brooke, think back to when we were students. I don't remember celibacy being high on our list of recreational alternatives. Do you honestly believe these kids are any different?''

She could feel the color rising, hot and revealing, in her cheeks. Unwilling to trust her voice at this point, she didn't answer him.

"Hell, for that matter they're not kids," Donovan added irritably. "They're grown men and women who are more than capable of making their own sexual decisions. If you're honestly afraid that we'd be single-handedly corrupting the entire student body, sweetheart, you can relax."

Donovan knew he was handling this badly, but now that he'd begun, he couldn't seem to stop. His green eyes speared hers. "Or is there something else you're afraid of?" he asked softly.

Brooke got up quickly, unwilling to continue this conversation. "I'll see what I can find for dinner."

Donovan rose to his feet, as well. Tilting her head back to look up at him, Brooke wondered why she had never noticed the vast discrepancy in their height before. Perhaps because he had never seemed so dangerous. So threatening.

"Don't bother. I've lost my appetite," he said flatly. He took her by the shoulders, holding her to his intense scrutiny. "Over these past years, whenever I thought about us, I always felt that I was to blame. That I hadn't paid enough attention to you, or that in trying to be fair, I'd ended up causing us both grief."

"I've already told you that I don't want to talk about the past," she insisted.

His fingers tightened their hold as his eyes narrowed dangerously. "And I've repeatedly told you that I do, that it's high time we got things out in the open. So where the hell does that leave us?"

Brooke jerked free. "I don't know," she whispered. She began gathering up her scattered clothing.

Donovan reached out a hand. "Brooke, be reasonable," he said tiredly. "What, exactly, is it you want from me?"

She clutched her black cocktail dress to her breasts as her eyes scanned the floor for her discarded panty hose. When she realized Donovan was still waiting for an answer, she moistened her lips.

"I don't know."

"But you do know that you're not willing to move in here with me."

Brooke's lips were drier than they had ever been in her life. "I can't."

Donovan closed his eyes on a slow, accepting blink. When he opened them, the anger had burned away, leaving only tenderness.

"Fine. Then let's get married."

"Married?"

He nodded. "Married. You and I."

"You and I?" she echoed.

Again the slight nod of his dark head. "As in man and wife. Spoon and June. And don't forget the best part—honeymoon."

Brooke went decidedly pale. "This isn't anything to joke about."

His level gaze refused to release hers. "So who's joking? We've put it off twelve long years, Brooke. I'd say that was long enough."

She shook her head. "I don't need those words. I made love with you of my own free will because I wanted you. And because you wanted me. You were right when you said things hadn't changed; what we shared the past two weeks has been incredible. But it's been sex, pure and simple. It isn't necessary to pretty it up with romantic pledges that you have no intention of keeping."

He resisted the urge to smile at her solemn expression, knowing that she would only accuse him of taking her words too lightly. "Is it that frightening?" he asked quietly.

Frightening. How strange that Donovan, who had always appeared blithely ignorant of her feelings, should hit upon the precise word. She wondered when he had switched his brilliant analytical skills to humans.

"Is what that frightening?" she whispered.

His green eyes offered steady reassurance. "Me loving you."

"It's too soon," she protested.

He brushed his lips lightly, lingeringly, against hers. "No, it's not."

As she found herself becoming beguiled by the gentle kiss, Brooke jerked her head back. "I can't handle this right now," she complained. "I've just moved to Claremont; I have a new apartment that's in desperate need of furniture, a new office that I've finally gotten into some semblance of order, and a new job that makes everything else I've done so far in my life look like child's play. Nearly every member of the faculty has been treating me as if I'm Typhoid Mary, and I know they're calling me horrible names behind my back."

She took a deep breath before continuing. "Until the party this evening, except for a few brief professional contacts, like President Chambers and Mrs. Harrigan, I didn't even know anyone here but you. And Gloria," she tacked on, thinking back on how she had actually enjoyed her brief conversation with Donovan's *Gorilla gorilla beringei*.

"And the last thing you need right now is another person making demands on you."

"That's about it," she agreed shakily.

"I'll give you some time to make up your mind," Donovan said as he touched her cheek. "In fact, it would probably be a good idea if we don't see each other for a few days. But don't take too long," he warned. "I'm not a patient man."

Not patient? This was the man who had taught a gorilla more than twelve hundred words, all the time ignoring the naysayers who insisted that such a feat was impossible? Brooke could recall Donovan's struggles to teach his chimps even the most rudimentary of conversational skills. Not patient?

"I find that difficult to believe," she murmured.

He cupped her chin. "Believe it," he said quietly before plucking her lacy black slip from the post at the end of the bed.

Brooke accepted the item of apparel with trembling hands, feeling like a coward as she retreated to the bathroom to dress. When she came out, Donovan was gone.

Donovan sat on his front porch, eyeing the dark windows of the neighboring house thoughtfully. Obviously Serena and Alex had gone to bed. For a brief moment he considered waking them up; he needed conversation, the comfort offered by individuals who honestly cared for him. People who loved him. Family.

Muttering a soft oath, he rose from the glider, shoving his hands deeply into his pockets as he left the porch and headed in the direction of the primate center. There was no point in burdening Serena with his troubles. She had enough on her mind with the upcoming Australian Open.

Donovan was traveling to Melbourne during the Thanksgiving break to watch his sister achieve her Grand Slam. Over the past two weeks, whenever he thought about the trip, he had automatically pictured Brooke by his side, sharing his days, and even more importantly, his nights. Now he was forced to reconsider that idea. There was an outside chance she wouldn't come.

"The hell she won't," he muttered as he unlocked the door to the gorilla compound. "She'll come to Australia if I have to drag her there by the hair."

He couldn't resist a grim smile at the thought of how Brooke would respond to such Neanderthal tactics. A wet cat was the first image that came to mind.

The apes were all asleep, with the exception of Gloria, who was, as usual, wide awake, her gaze locked onto a television screen distorted by wide, fuzzy horizontal black bars.

"Hi," Donovan greeted her, pulling up a chair.

She gave him an impatient sign. "Where new television?"

Donovan sighed, thinking that he couldn't seem to please any of the women in his life lately. "I'm working on it." He signed his words as he answered. "What are we watching?"

Her broad sloping forehead furrowed into deep scowl lines. "Gloria watch bang bang shooting. You no watch. Donovan bad."

"So I've been told," he muttered. He crossed the room to the refrigerator where he took out a jar of peanut butter, another jar of strawberry jelly and a loaf of whole-wheat bread. "Want something to eat?" he asked over his shoulder.

Gleaming black eyes observed him suspiciously. "Snack? Now?"

Breaking Gloria's strict regime was admittedly unusual behavior. But it didn't seem polite to eat one of her favorite sandwiches in front of her without offering her something to eat as well.

"Now," he agreed.

The gorilla didn't wait to be asked twice. "Jell-O," she ordered. "Red. And cookie." When Donovan didn't object, the huge ape apparently decided to take advantage of this extraordinary occasion. "Two cookies. Oreos."

"Two cookies coming up."

Donovan knew that he was probably creating a monster. Tomorrow night Gloria would undoubtedly insist on a midnight snack. He shook his head, refusing to take on any more problems than he already had for the time being.

He prepared his own sandwich, then gave Gloria a bowl of strawberry Jell-O, her favorite flavor, and two Oreo cookies. As always, he was amazed by the delicacy of the gorilla's huge hands as she took the cookies apart, her wide yellow teeth scraping at the soft frosting center.

"So," he signed as he sat down to watch *The Untouchables*, which while black and white, was at least in English for a change, "why are you mad at me?"

"Donovan bad. Donovan not come night. Gloria lonely."

"I was here during dinner," he argued.

Admittedly he hadn't stayed as long as he would have liked, but there had been the party to go to. After that, he had taken Brooke back to his house, and for a while, it looked as if he was going to spend the night in her arms.

Gloria eyed him accusingly. "You not come put Gloria sleep. Not many nights."

"I've been busy."

Gloria appeared not to have heard Donovan's response as she remained outwardly engrossed in the television set. Finally, when the program broke for a commercial featuring a used-car dealer who routinely broke windshields with a sledgehammer in order to wake up the late-night audience, she turned back toward him.

"Busy what? Getting new television?"

"Trying to." It was the first lie he'd ever told her and it made him feel like a heel.

She flashed a forgiving grin. "Gloria like new television," she signed as the G-men returned to the screen.

As Eliot Ness smashed up a speakeasy, Donovan wondered what he was going to do if Brooke turned down his grant proposal. There was one alternative, he considered. But for the present he preferred to keep that possibility as a last resort. Donovan could only hope that Brooke wouldn't push him into it.

If Brooke thought the long weekend without Donovan had stretched out interminably, the following week passed by no less slowly. While the unexpected free time gave her the opportunity to finish settling into her apartment, as well as completing the redecoration of her office, she still found herself gazing out the window, searching for a glimpse of him.

With her evenings now free, she resumed the nightly running that had always kept unwanted pounds from her hips. Initially she had been tempted to choose a route that would take her past Donovan's house, but had ultimately rejected that idea. The man might be obtuse when it came to interpersonal relationships, but Brooke knew that even Donovan would be capable of seeing through such shallow subterfuge.

Late Friday afternoon, one week after their argument, Brooke was staring intently out the window, as if it might be possible to conjure Donovan up by sheer mental effort. How she missed him! A student tossed a Frisbee to his dog on the lawn outside her window, the Irish setter leaping higher and higher with each succeeding catch, but Brooke was only aware of dog and owner on the most absent of levels as she wondered why these past few days apart were proving even more painful than the intervening years had been.

Before she could come up with an answer to that vexing question, the intercom on her desk buzzed, announcing the arrival of her next appointment.

Brooke rose as the visitor entered her office. Tall, perpetually tanned, with swept-back silver hair, General Langley Osborne, U.S. Air Force, retired, made an impressive entrance. His three-piece navy suit, while a departure from the uniform the general usually wore, was expensive and impeccably tailored. A burgundy tie provided a splash of color against the pristine white shirt, the bright hue echoed by the pocket handkerchief worn at his breast. His black shoes were polished to gleaming jet.

"Miss Stirling," General Osborne greeted her in a booming, oratorical voice that he used even in the most casual of conversations, "I'm sorry that I wasn't able to meet with you along with the others." He gave her a broad, professional smile. "Priorities, you know."

Behind the tinted aviator glasses, his gray eyes moved from the top of her dark head down to her black snakeskin pumps. "However, if I had known what an attractive young woman Brad Chambers had brought in to administer our funds, I would have told the president that he'd have to find someone else to chair his meetings on space systems defenses."

The legendary man was as smooth in person as he was on all those television news programs. Brooke knew the general was not referring to President Chambers. No, this was the nation's chief executive he was mentioning so casually. She smiled.

"I certainly wouldn't want to interfere with the inner workings of our government."

His eyes narrowed almost imperceptibly. "Wouldn't you?" he inquired, pointedly ignoring her outstretched hand.

If Brooke thought that subtle accusation was to be a low point in their discussion, she was to be proven wrong. During the next forty-five minutes, the meeting continued to slide progressively downhill. She was more than a little relieved when the general glanced down at his gold Rolex watch and professed another appointment. Breathing a deep sigh, she kicked off her shoes, folded her arms on her desk and lowered her forehead to them.

"You look like a lady who could use a hot fudge sundae." A deep, wonderfully familiar voice broke into her weary thoughts.

Brooke lifted her head. "With extra nuts?"

Donovan nodded. "Of course."

"And marshmallow crème?"

"Could I forget the marshmallow crème? And three, count them, three maraschino cherries."

He pulled the cardboard container from behind his back. "Peace offering," he announced.

"I hadn't realized we were at war," she murmured as she dug into the gooey delight.

He claimed a chair across from her and stretched his long legs out in front of him. "Not war," he amended. "I suppose it's been more like an armed truce. Speaking of arms," he said offhandedly, "how did you get along with the Great One? I saw him marching out of the building as I came in."

She shrugged. "About as well as can be expected. He made some not so subtle references to the state of the nation, friends in high places, that sort of thing."

"But he didn't stoop to begging you to leave his budget intact."

She managed a weak smile at that. "Donovan, the man has been military advisor to three presidents. Not only is he a regular on *Face the Nation*, *Meet the Press*, and *The MacNeil/Lehrer Report*, he pops up at least once a week on *Nightline*. His name is a household word and I doubt if you could find many people who wouldn't recognize his face."

"I read a poll a few months back that said more people could identify the general than the vice president."

Brooke nodded. "That's precisely what I mean. The name General Langley Osborne is synonymous with power. Do you think a man like that would beg a nobody like me for anything?"

"Probably not." His eyes narrowed as he took in the distress Brooke was trying hard to conceal. "You're going to do it, aren't you?" he said with a sense of wonder and just a little awe. "You're going to cut his budget right along with the rest of us peons."

"You know I can't reveal that information," she protested quietly. There was no need to. Her trembling fingers, as she lined up a row of pencils, gave her away.

"Well, I sure hope you've got a start on your fallout shelter," he said easily. "Because you're going to need one before this is over."

Brooke mumbled a vague agreement as she turned her attention to the dessert Donovan had brought her. A comfortable silence settled over them and Donovan used the time to study her refurbished office. She had done wonders with the place. Everything about the small office spoke of money and good taste, from the soft plush of the gray and blue Oriental rug, which had replaced the original tobacco-brown carpeting, to the Impressionist paintings on the blue-gray walls.

"I like what you've done," he commented. "I'd heard you were efficient, but no one ever mentioned that you were a miracle worker."

Brooke's gaze drifted around the room. "If I had known you were dropping by, I'd have instructed Mrs. Harrigan to toss today's correspondence around a little to make you feel more at home."

His brows rose. "Is that any way to talk to a man who brings you hot fudge sundaes?" he chided softly.

Brooke lowered her lashes as she stirred the chocolate sauce and melted vanilla ice cream mixture with the red plastic spoon Donovan had supplied. "I'm sorry," she said quietly. "You're right, that was a cheap shot."

He crossed his legs, bracing an ankle over his knee. "I don't know," he murmured, "I think I like the idea of you acting out of character. It tends to give a man the impression that you might care. Just a little?"

Brooke met his questioning gaze with a wary one of her own. "I do. More than a little."

His answering smile, while revealing satisfaction, did not appear to gloat. "That makes two of us." He leaned back, linking his fingers behind his head as he observed her thoughtfully. "So, where does that leave us?"

Brooke shook her head. "I don't know."

"Would it surprise you to know that I've been giving the matter a great deal of thought this past week? And that while I haven't come to any definite conclusions, I do have an inkling of what may be part of our problem."

"What's that?"

"Our past is messing up our future."

She stiffened. "If you're talking about the way things ended—"

He held up a hand. "No, I'm not," he said. Then he smiled slightly. "Well, that obviously can't be discounted, but it's not what I'm referring to. I think part of our problem comes from the fact that since the physical attraction has remained as strong as ever, we assumed everything else would be the same, too."

Brooke was beginning to follow Donovan's train of thought and had to admit he could have stumbled onto something. "So we automatically fell into old habits even though we're not the same people we once were."

He gave her a congratulatory look. "Exactly. We became lovers before we became friends."

Brooke took a bite of her sundae, relishing the combination of hot fudge and chilled ice cream on her tongue as she considered Donovan's words. "You could be right."

"I was hoping you'd agree," he said, trying hard not to display too much masculine satisfaction. It had not been easy for him to stay away from Brooke for an entire week, but he had convinced himself that his goals would be more easily achieved if she were forced to see that a lifetime alone was not nearly as appealing as the one they could share together. Right now, all Donovan wanted to do was to take Brooke back home to his bed. Where she belonged.

Brooke scraped the last of the melted ice cream from the bottom of the dish. "I do." She leaned back in her chair, swiveling absently from side to side. "Although I'm amazed that you would have so much insight to the human condition."

"Hey," Donovan complained, appearing boyishly aggrieved, "don't forget, I'm supposed to be the hotshot primate specialist. And while you are definitely worlds more appealing than Gloria and the rest of her clan, you do still technically fit into that category, Brooke."

"How kind of you to point that out," she said dryly.

He grinned as he rose from the chair. "Any time. Ready to go?"

"Go? Where?"

It was Donovan's turn to look confused. "Home, of course." Remembering what had started this argument in the first place, he backpedaled in an attempt to be scrupulously fair this time. "Or if you'd rather, we can spend tonight at your place."

Brooke had been in the process of putting her shoes back on, but at his words, she stopped to glance up at him curiously.

"Let me get this straight," she said slowly. "You believe, and for the record, I happen to agree with you, that we jumped into this relationship too rapidly. That we began sleeping together without discovering who the other person really was."

"That's it in a nutshell," he agreed. "Do you need help with that shoe?"

"I need assistance understanding how such a brilliant man could make such a quantum leap in logic," she countered. "Obviously, Donovan, we have to stop making love."

"What?"

He stared at her, dumbfounded, wondering what he could have possibly said to have made Brooke jump to such an erroneous conclusion. That unattractive solution had been the furthest thing from his mind. He came around the desk.

"It's really quite simple," Brooke said. "Actually, I don't understand why I didn't think of it myself. It's obvious that we're basing all our understanding of each other on the idea of who we were twelve years ago. It would also stand to reason that not only are those memories colored with certain prejudices, they also don't reflect who we are today."

He ran his palm along her shoulder, coaxing the tense muscles under his touch to relax. "Agreed. But what does that have to do with us making love?"

Brooke shrugged off his hand as she tugged on the black snakeskin pump. "Our only intimacy has been in bed. We've made a lot of love, Donovan, but that doesn't mean we know anything about each other."

His long fingers curled around her upper arms as he lifted her from the chair. "We'll talk," he said against her hair as he drew her into his arms. "You'll fill in all the gaps, then it'll be my turn." He ran his hands down her back, cupping her hips to draw her into an intimate embrace. "Then we'll make love. All night long."

Brooke felt herself responding to the seduction of his hands, the purr of his words as he nibbled at her ear, the strength of his body pressing against hers. It would be so easy to simply succumb to this sensual moment. But if she allowed herself to slip this time, how would things ever change between them?

"I don't think that's a good idea." Her hands pushed lightly against his shoulders. "And it's definitely not what I mean."

Donovan brushed his lips against her temple. "You've lost me, Brooke. Was I wrong to think that you've missed me as much these past days as I have you? Wasn't your bed as cold and lonely as mine? Your life as empty? Didn't you find yourself waking up in the middle of the night, wanting me?"

"Of course I wanted you," she said on a soft moan as his hand slid between them to cup her breast.

"And now you're going to have me," he soothed, his lips plucking enticingly at hers. "We'll both have what we want, sweetheart."

Her head was swimming, her bones were melting, and her resolve was spinning dangerously out of reach. Brooke forced herself to break the warming contact.

"No," she insisted. "This isn't what I want."

"Isn't it?" he challenged softly.

"No," Brooke repeated, strengthening her voice as well as her determination.

"Are you saying that we're not going to see each other again?"

"Of course I'm not," Brooke protested. "Besides, that would be a little difficult, wouldn't it? After all, I do have a year's contract with the college. And you're certainly not going anywhere."

"Don't be so sure of that," he said under his breath.

Brooke's gaze suddenly sharpened. "What does that mean?"

Donovan's only response was a slight shrug. "Nothing. Getting back to our relationship, are you by any chance suggesting that we keep things strictly on a business basis?''

Brooke put her hands behind her back to prevent him from viewing her nervous fingers as they twisted together. This wasn't going to be easy. Donovan's naturally amiable face could have been carved from granite.

''Not exactly. Unless you want to keep it that way.''

''Of course I don't!''

''Neither do I,'' she admitted. ''But I think we ought to take things one step at a time. Get to know each other on some other level besides sex.''

He appeared honestly taken aback by her proposal. ''Are you suggesting we date?''

''It's not exactly a dirty word, Donovan. Believe it or not, men and women actually manage to enjoy each other's company from time to time without ending up in the bedroom.''

''Dating's for kids,'' he objected.

''So think of it as remaining young at heart,'' Brooke countered calmly.

Donovan opted for logic. ''Honey, be reasonable. There's no reason why we can't share more of our lives and our feelings, but I don't see that giving up a terrific sex life is going to prove anything.'' His gaze was suddenly sharp. ''You do enjoy that part, don't you? I mean, you wouldn't fake it or anything?''

Brooke reached up and patted his cheek. ''Of course not. No one has ever made me feel the way you do, Donovan.''

''At least that's something,'' he muttered, obviously aggrieved. ''But if you feel that way, why do you want to make us both suffer? Are you attempting to live up to some ridiculously romanticized hearts-and-flowers ideal that only happens in novels? Or schmaltzy movies?''

Brooke had forgotten that Donovan could be so patronizing. "Don't talk to me as if you're the intelligent, lucid scientist and I'm the emotional, irrational female. I'll have you know that hundreds, thousands—" she waved her hand to encompass the entire world outside her window "—*millions* of people share my feelings."

"I hadn't realized we'd called for a referendum."

She glared up at him. "You don't have to be sarcastic."

"And you don't have to be so intransigent. Be reasonable, Brooke, you're not just insisting we start all over again, you're asking me to forget everything I've learned about you."

His eyes gleamed as they moved over her face. "You want me to deny that your soft scent fills my head like an inhaled drug. You're insisting that I pretend I haven't noticed that your lustrous eyes widen and turn to gold when I enter you. You're asking me to ignore the fact that your skin is soft as satin and gleams in the moonlight with the iridescence of natural pearls—"

"Stop that!"

Donovan tilted his head. "See what I mean?" he asked with a challenging smile. "You can't put it out of your mind any better than I can."

"Of course I can," Brooke snapped.

"Really?" He held out his arms. "Come kiss me and tell me that."

Brooke stayed where she was. "I didn't say it was going to be easy. But it's something that I'm going to insist on, Donovan."

He dropped one arm to his side. The long fingers of his other hand rubbed his chin. "What happens if I don't agree?"

"That's your privilege," she said, turning away, unable to meet his gaze.

A moment later she heard him sigh. "Well, I don't seem to have any choice, so I suppose I'll have to go along with it. For now."

She spun around, giving him a grateful smile. "Thank you, Donovan." Her tone, as well as her expression, was unusually formal. "I appreciate you making the effort."

He ran his index finger down her nose. "For now," he repeated firmly. "And don't think that I'm not going to try to change your mind, sexy lady," he warned.

Knowing that Donovan was at least willing to meet her halfway gave Brooke the courage to face his challenge. "There's nothing you can possibly do that will make any difference."

He rocked forward on the balls of his feet, planting a swift, hard kiss against her firmly set lips. "Before I'm finished you'll not only be pleading for me to make love to you, Brooke Stirling, you'll also be begging me to marry you."

Incensed at the latent humor in his tone, Brooke jerked her head back. "I've already proposed to you once, Donovan," she flared. "What on earth makes you think I'd make a fool of myself again?"

He grinned down at her, appearing unperturbed by her sudden flash of temper. "The first time you brought the subject up, I had other things on my mind." He brushed his knuckles up her flushed cheek, leaving sparks on her skin. "Believe me, sweetheart, this time you'll have my full attention."

He turned on his heel, heading toward her office door. "By the way, the weatherman says this Indian summer is going to hold through the weekend. How would you like to go on a picnic tomorrow?''

"I don't know if that's such a good idea."

As appealing as the prospect sounded, Brooke knew that to be all alone with Donovan, in some secluded wooded glen, could present a myriad of tempting situations. Several that she wasn't certain she was up to resisting, despite her brave words.

As if reading her mind, he winked knowingly. "Don't worry. I'll bring along a chaperon."

"Promise?"

He appeared affronted. "I have every intention of seducing you, Brooke. But that doesn't mean that I'd lie to you to achieve that goal." He gave her a dazzling, self-assured grin. "I won't have to."

His dark head cleared the doorway a moment before the ledger book hit the frame. Glaring at the spot where he had stood so smugly only moments before, Brooke could hear Donovan's hearty chuckle as he strode jauntily down the hall.

Chapter Nine

To Brooke's amazement, Donovan actually showed up on time at her apartment the following morning. Opening the door, she greeted him with a rewarding smile.

"Good morning. Would you like a cup of coffee before we go?"

"Sorry, but I'd better not."

He appeared strangely distracted. Having spent an inordinate amount of time preparing for a simple Saturday picnic, Brooke had been expecting a compliment on her appearance. Instead, Donovan kept casting nervous glances back down the hallway.

"Donovan, are you all right?"

"Sure," he said, giving her a rather harried smile. "Are you ready to go?"

Brooke combed her fingers distractedly through her hair. Something was very, very wrong. "Just let me turn off the coffeepot, and I will be."

He clapped his hands together. "Great. Why don't I just wait downstairs in the parking lot?"

Brooke opened her mouth to ask Donovan how long he thought it was going to take her to switch off a simple kitchen appliance, but he was already jogging back down the hallway. Puzzled, she went into the kitchen, flipped the switch on the electric coffeemaker, rinsed out the Pyrex pot and put it in the dishwasher. Casting a quick, critical glance around the spotless kitchen, she left the apartment.

Brooke found Donovan in the parking lot, as promised, standing beside a blue and white van. "I don't believe it," she exclaimed as she viewed the familiar face peering at her from a captain's chair in the back of the van.

"I told you I was bringing along a chaperon."

"You certainly did," Brooke agreed. "But you conveniently forgot to mention that said chaperon just happened to be a two-hundred-pound gorilla."

His brow furrowed. "I didn't think to ask if you'd mind. Do you?"

Brooke waggled a hello with her fingers to Gloria. "Not at all. If nothing else, it'll give me a chance to catch up with what's happening on *Hill Street Blues*." She went to open the passenger door.

"Just one minute, lady," Donovan objected.

She glanced back over her shoulder. "Something wrong?"

"You haven't kissed me good morning."

"I know." She turned away again.

"Uh-uh." Donovan's touch was light but firm as he caught Brooke's shoulders and pulled her into his arms. "Have I told you yet today that you look lovely?"

"No," she said, trying to keep the sulky tone from her voice.

His gaze moved from the top of her shiny dark hair, down over her russet cotton sweater and indigo jeans, to her feet, sensibly clad in running shoes. Donovan decided that as beautiful as Brooke appeared in those stylish suits and silk dresses she wore to work, he preferred her in casual clothing. She appeared softer. And worlds more approachable.

"Then I was decidedly remiss. You are beautiful."

His husky tone caused Brooke to pluck nervously at a nonexistent thread on the sleeve of her sweater. "Thank you."

"I was incredibly, miserably lonely last night. How about you?"

The warm, emerald glow of his eyes was heating her skin, belying the crisp September morning temperature. "I kept busy," she murmured, her attention riveted to a distant spot beyond his shoulder.

"Busy enough not to think about how your body warms to my touch?" He ran his palms down the back of her thighs. "Were you able to keep from remembering how your pulse leaps when I touch you here?" His fingers brushed her breasts. "And here?" He pressed his palm against her stomach. "And here?"

Brooke jerked away before the treacherous hand could move any lower. "You promised," she accused in a voice trembling with an uneasy blend of desire and anger.

"I promised to seduce you," he countered gruffly, tangling his fingers in her hair as he held her to a long, luxurious kiss.

Donovan's open mouth swallowed Brooke's words of protest, his tongue probing arrogantly, claiming the dark recesses behind her teeth. As a singeing heat surged through her veins, Brooke reminded herself that for the moment, she was safe. Donovan would never actually attempt to make love to her here in the parking lot. And the van was already conveniently—or inconveniently, depending on one's point of view—occupied by a rather intimidating deterrent.

Since he obviously couldn't leave Gloria alone in the van in order to return to Brooke's apartment, she was free to allow herself the pleasure of this single kiss. Her hands clung to the solid plane of his shoulders as she rose onto her toes, pressing her body against him, delighting in his resultant growl of masculine pleasure.

"I knew you couldn't deny it," he said finally, burying his lips in her hair.

"Deny what?" she murmured, distracted by the soft, rosy cloud fogging her mind.

"That with us, sex is inevitable."

At his smug, self-satisfied explanation, Brooke came crashing back to earth. "You cheated!"

He grinned down at her. "I never said I wouldn't cheat, sweetheart. If I recall, I only promised not to lie."

She shook her head with reluctant admiration for his ingenuous reasoning. "I don't know what I see in you, Donovan Kincaid."

He ran his hand down her back, causing a flutter of desire to skim along the delicate bones of her spine. "Don't you?"

Brooke looked past him at the gorilla seated in the back seat. "Don't you think we'd better join your friend? Before she gets the notion to join us?"

"Good idea," Donovan agreed reluctantly. "Although she'd probably be content to sing along with Springsteen for a little longer."

Brooke's eyes narrowed as she focused on Gloria. A pair of earphones spanned the wide ebony head. "Springsteen?"

Donovan nodded. "She's had a crush on the guy ever since she accidentally caught one of his videos on the rock music station while flipping around the dial looking for a cop show."

"I refuse to believe that."

He lifted his right hand. "Honest. Stephanie thought it was kind of cute, so she bought Gloria a cassette player and a couple of tapes." He grimaced in a way that gave Brooke the distinct impression that he wasn't pulling her leg, after all. "I pitched in for the earphones after listening to 'Born to Run' for six straight hours."

"I'll say this for you, Donovan," Brooke remarked as she climbed into the front passenger seat of the van. "You certainly have more interesting friends than most of the men I've gone out with."

As he fastened his seat belt, Donovan arched a challenging brow. "Most?"

Brooke laughed. "All," she admitted, watching as the great ape's head moved back and forth to the driving rock beat.

Gloria immediately sat up a little straighter, eyeing Brooke with renewed interest. "You bring new television?"

"Did you by any chance set this up?" Brooke asked Donovan suspiciously after he'd translated Gloria's opening question.

"Not at all. Gloria's been accusing me of neglecting her lately, so I promised her an outing if it stayed sunny through the weekend. I thought you might enjoy a day in the country, as well."

When he appeared to be telling the truth, Brooke felt just the slightest bit guilty. "It'll definitely be different from the way I usually spend my Saturdays."

"That's what I figured," he said simply.

A comfortable silence settled over the van as Donovan took the San Bernardino freeway out of town. Brooke noticed that Gloria, absorbed in the passing scenery, remained quietly in her seat, her gorilla head bobbing in time to the music only she could hear. From time to time she engaged in a little back-seat driving, leaning forward to tap Donovan on the shoulder, signing for him to take an exit.

"She loves banana milk shakes," he explained to Brooke as Gloria indicated that she wouldn't object to a stop at a roadside Dairy Queen. "We'll stop on the way back," he informed the gorilla, who appeared willing to accept that compromise.

"Where are we going?" Brooke asked, after they had been driving about thirty minutes.

"The college owns a ranch up in the hill country. They use it for retreats, things like that. I try to take Gloria up there at least once a month so that she can run free."

He looked up at the rearview mirror, smiling at the ape's reflection. "It's a real treat to watch her acting like a real gorilla. And not some laboratory experiment."

Brooke glanced back at the gorilla. At the moment she appeared engrossed in a child's picture book. "Bad," Gloria signed, holding the book up for Brooke's perusal. "Bad wolf. Break house." She shook her head. "Poor pig," she signed dramatically. "So sad."

"Actually," Brooke said, after Donovan had translated for her, "I'd say you treat her a lot more like a pampered child than a laboratory experiment."

"That's what Serena says," he agreed conversationally. "She's decided that I'm overcompensating with Gloria because I've never had any kids of my own."

That thought hadn't occurred to Brooke. Now that it did, she found it rather interesting to consider Donovan as a father. He certainly wouldn't be an orthodox one, she decided.

"Is there any truth to her accusation?"

He shrugged. "Serena's got kids on the mind these days."

"Oh?"

Gloria began drawing enthusiastic squiggles over the pages of her book with a pencil she had found on the floor of the van. Brooke decided not to interfere with the impromptu art session.

"Alex's best friend's wife gave birth to their first child in July, so he and Serena spent the latter half of the summer in Washington adoring Alex's reportedly brilliant godson. On top of that, Serena claims that as soon as she wins the Australian Open, she's planning to tie Alex to the bed until he provides her with an heir to the Lawrence tennis title."

"Does she intend to keep playing?"

Donovan changed lanes, weaving his way through the weekend traffic. "Obviously she'll have to take some time off while she's pregnant. Then she's got this master plan figured out that calls for her to only accept tournaments scheduled during Alex's breaks. That way they can take the baby with them."

"They say travel is broadening for a child."

He nodded, flipping on the turn signal. "That's what they say, all right." He glanced over at her as they left the freeway, turning onto a two-lane highway. "What about you?"

"I've always enjoyed traveling," Brooke allowed, purposely misunderstanding his question.

Not taking the hint, Donovan pressed on. "I meant do you ever think about having kids?"

She took a sudden interest in the trees flashing by the passenger window. "Sometimes."

"And?"

Brooke reminded herself that the entire point of this new phase of their relationship was to allow her and Donovan a chance to get to know each other. Recalling how her lack of candor had contributed to their breakup, she decided to be open with her feelings.

"It's funny, when I was young, I didn't want any children. I wanted to be free to live my own life without being tied down like my mother was."

Donovan nodded. "I can understand that. After all, yours was the first generation of women to really be given a choice between motherhood and a career. I guess it was inevitable that not everyone would want to follow in their mothers' footsteps."

"I suppose so," Brooke said. "And then, after I was married, it seemed that there was never time to even bring up the subject of a child. Let alone take care of one if we had decided to give parenthood a try."

"There are some distinct disadvantages to being a workaholic," he said knowingly.

It was odd, but over the past year Donovan had found himself experiencing occasional yearnings for a family. Serena had steadfastly insisted that all the painting and fix-up work he had done to his house this past year was nothing more than a human version of nest preparation. He had laughed it off at the time, but since Brooke's return to Claremont, those vague feelings had crystallized into a strong desire for a fuller life than that offered by his work.

"I know," Brooke agreed on a soft sigh. "I suppose if I hadn't been so set upon making a success of my career, I'd still be married today."

"Surely your husband knew you intended to work when he married you." Donovan hated Brooke's former husband without even knowing the man. It was galling to think of some other man living with her, loving with her.

Brooke thought she detected a touch of anger in Donovan's tone. She wondered if she had said something to irritate him but a surreptitious glance at his profile revealed nothing.

"Peter thought he could change my mind. Unfortunately he and I had entirely different ideas of what we wanted our lives to be. He wanted a woman like his mother. Like my mother."

"I see," Donovan murmured, unable to imagine any man desiring a clone of Carolyn Stirling for a wife. The woman was so frigid, so unfeeling, she'd undoubtedly create a layer of frost on the sheets.

Once again Brooke was left to wonder if she had only imagined Donovan's rough, half-angry tone. "Anyway, my work began taking more and more of the time Peter felt I should be spending to help advance his own career by giving parties, playing bridge, that sort of thing."

"I don't remember you playing bridge."

She wrinkled her nose. "If you were to ask Peter, he'd tell you that I don't. Despite his efforts to teach me the subtleties of the game, I proved to be a distinct disappointment."

Donovan reached across the small space between their seats to take her hand. "Any man who'd be disappointed with you would have to be a damned fool."

Brooke looked down at their joined hands, wondering how such a casual touch could cause her heart to beat a little faster.

"Peter was a brilliant stockbroker. His family had known mine forever."

"So you married the guy in order to make all the relatives happy?"

"Not exactly." Brooke took a sudden interest in locating a radio station. Soon the soft sounds of a popular singer crooning a romantic ballad filled the air. "I loved Peter," she insisted quietly. "I really did."

Donovan wondered who Brooke was trying harder to convince—herself or him. But he remained silent, encouraging her to continue. The fact that Brooke was willing to share her past with him was a decided step forward.

"Everyone thought we had the perfect marriage." She moved her shoulders in a sad, little shrug. "That's what we wanted them to think. Heaven knows, if we'd put half as much time into working out our differences as we did to maintaining appearances, we might have made it work."

"Think so?" he asked with studied casualness.

"No," Brooke said on a soft, rippling sigh. "Not really. Peter and I had different dreams. Contrary goals."

Failure. Even now, the cold, dark feeling flooded over her. Brooke shook her head, fighting off lingering memories that she thought she had put behind her. Unaccustomed to personal defeat, Brooke couldn't help wondering if the fact that she had made a mess of two important relationships was proof that she was not meant to share her life with anyone.

"I never could live up to his expectations."

Donovan squeezed her fingers. "It was his loss."

As Brooke returned the pressure on her hand, she managed a half smile. "I don't remember this talent of yours for saying precisely the right thing."

He lifted their linked hands to his lips. "I'm only saying what I feel, Brooke."

She studied his face in silence. As his green eyes swept over her features, warming her skin, it was all she could do to keep her gaze level. She was relieved when the suspended moment passed and Donovan returned his attention to his driving.

"I believe we were discussing our lack of progeny," he stated offhandedly as he pulled out to pass a slow-moving tractor.

His statement, while casual, carried the lingering weight of a command. Brooke figured that she'd gone this far, she might as well continue.

"When Peter and I finally gave in to the inevitable and divorced, I'll admit to being relieved that we'd never had a child. If I'd had to carry all the burdens of being a single mother, along with my work, I'd probably be one of a faceless sea of accountants stuck behind a desk in some enormous, impersonal corporation."

"You've achieved a great deal in such a short time," he agreed quietly, wondering if Brooke was trying to explain that she had no desire for children.

"I suppose I have. But after a few years something happened. I don't know if it was my biological clock ticking away, or if I was beginning to realize that I was never going to leave anything permanent behind, but I started thinking more and more about children."

She studied her fingernails, unwilling to meet the curious gaze she could feel directed her way. "I began stopping by the park a few blocks from my apartment to watch the children play. The more I thought about it, the more I decided that I wanted it all—a houseful of kids, a husband and a career."

She glanced over at him cautiously. "Does that sound selfish to you?"

Donovan's smile was quick, warm and reassuring. "Not at all. In fact, to tell you the truth, I'm relieved. I've always liked the idea of being a father. But I didn't want to push you into anything."

"You're back to the crazy idea of us getting married."

"Of course." His smile remained totally guileless. "Better hold on to your seat, the going gets a little rough from here on in."

Brooke opened her mouth to inform him that in the first place, they weren't getting married. And in the second, she had become resigned to the idea that motherhood wasn't in the cards for her. It had been six years since she'd taken to watching children. In that entire time she had not met one likely prospect to complete her ideal image of a happy family.

Over the years since her divorce, she had met a handful of men who would admittedly make wonderful parents. They had been kind, understanding and incredibly patient. But she hadn't fallen in love with any of them. As she entered her thirties, more and more of the men she met were divorced, already paying support for children of previous marriages. Those men, as a rule, were not looking to start new families. The only pitter-patter of little feet they were interested in hearing around their high-tech furnished bachelor apartments belonged to the nubile young women they invariably dated.

She wanted to explain all this to Donovan, but as he turned onto a bumpy gravel road, riddled with potholes, Brooke found conversation difficult, if not impossible. She fell silent, content to watch the signs of civilization slowly disappear to be replaced by the peaceful serenity of high grasslands.

Heaven. She was in heaven. Or at least the closest thing a mere mortal could come to it. The warm, sun-filled autumn day proved to be one of the most wonderful Brooke had ever known. As she watched Gloria romp around the ranch, free of restraints, Brooke wished that the day could go on forever.

Gloria dug enthusiastically in the soft dirt, excavating roots that she obviously found extremely tasty. She sunbathed, raided the picnic basket for fruit, and napped.

"I see what you mean," Brooke said thoughtfully as she and Donovan sat on a red-and-green-plaid blanket he had spread on the grass. Gloria was off frolicking in the trees, exactly as she might in her natural habitat. "It almost makes me want to kidnap her and set her free."

"I know the feeling." Donovan frowned as he peeled an orange. "It's damn unfortunate that her best prospect for survival should be under the protection of man. And man threatens to be the extinction of her species in the first place."

Brooke drew her knees up to her chest and wrapped her arms around them. "I don't understand."

"You probably noticed while studying my financial report that Gloria is mine. She doesn't belong to the college."

Brooke nodded. "Thanks," she said, accepting a slice of the ripe, succulent fruit. She savored the cool burst of flavor as she bit into it. "Actually, I did find that a bit odd. After all, the other apes are all college inventory."

"I was working with some chimps at Cornell," Donovan explained, "when a fellow scientist came to give a talk on her own work with a group of *Gorilla gorilla beringei* in the Virunga Mountains of Rwanda. That's in central Africa," he added at her questioning glance.

"Anyway, Karin had spent the last five years living with a family of gorillas and was convinced that although they were inferior to the chimpanzee in their ability to fashion tools and operate mechanisms, they were far superior in other aspects of behavioral adaptation.

"Since I'd been reading reports of her work, I was admittedly intrigued. Enough so that when she invited me to go back with her, I jumped at the chance."

"I can imagine," Brooke murmured.

He looked over at her curiously. "Are you by any chance jealous?"

"It depends. How old was this Karin person?"

"Twenty-eight."

Brooke scowled. "Terrific. Tell me she looked like Margaret Mead, and I'll forget I even brought the subject up."

"She was tall, blond and gave the best belch vocalization I've ever heard."

Brooke laughed, as she was supposed to. "Trust you to include that last one in a woman's attributes."

Donovan's fingers curved around the back of her neck as he leaned down to give her a brief kiss. "Karin was intelligent, attractive and shared my work, which was admittedly nice for a time," he said, his expression suddenly more serious than the light conversation warranted. "But she didn't make me crazy like you do, Brooke. And I never, ever, gave any consideration to marrying her."

Brooke plucked a dandelion from the grass, absently shredding its yellow blossom. "You were telling me about Gloria," she reminded him.

Anger flared briefly in his eyes. Then he sighed, turning his attention to the gorilla, who had climbed down from the tree and was presently lying on her back at the bottom of the slight hill, her broad abdomen turned upward toward the sun.

"The *Gorilla gorilla beringei* is a rare subspecies," he continued, "found only in the Virunga Mountains. Man's continual encroachment threatens their very survival. I doubt if Gloria's family will survive for many more generations."

"That's very sad."

"If you think that's sad, you should have seen what was left of Gloria's mother when the poachers got through with her. We found her body, the spears still in it, lying in the brush. Her head and hands had been hacked off for trophies."

Donovan's own hands curled into fists at his side. Brooke could hear the anger as well as the lingering pain in his voice and sought to banish the cause.

"It's all right," she said as she slowly uncurled his fingers to slip her hand into his. "You don't have to tell me any more if it's too painful."

He grunted. "I suppose that's when I discovered that I'm more suited for the lab than the bush. I wanted to go find the guys and kill them. Although Karin was admittedly angry, and even cried for a short time, she assured me that what I'd witnessed was nothing unusual. That such slaughter was a way of life."

"I suppose they left Gloria behind?" she asked, striving to find something pleasant about this tale.

He gave a harsh laugh, devoid of mirth. The sound sent a chill down Brooke's spine. "Not a chance. Karin insisted that we'd never find her, but I refused to believe that. I walked back to the nearest settlement and waited. Two weeks later, these jerks came into camp, carrying her in a potato basket. She was suffering from malnutrition and dehydration, her body had become dangerously emaciated and she had lost most of her hair."

A horrified gasp escaped Brooke's lips at the picture his words had created in her mind. She turned her eyes toward the happily snoozing Gloria, trying to coincide the vastly dissimilar images.

"What happened?"

His smile was grim. "They made the mistake of offering to sell her to me for a thousand dollars."

Brooke winced. "I'm not sure I want to know."

He took her finger and ran it down his nose. "Feel that?"

There was a definite thickening of the cartilage right below the bridge. "Uh-huh." Her eyes widened. "They broke your nose?"

This time his grin was broad and self-satisfied. "Yeah, but you should have seen the other guys."

"You didn't—" Brooke didn't quite know how to finish that question.

"Kill them?" Donovan shrugged his shoulders. "Nah. In the first place, even as furious as I was, I realized that I could get Karin's permit canceled if I went off half-cocked, committing murder and mayhem in her name. Also, to tell the truth, I don't think I have it in me to take another life. But," he added with undeniable pride, "I did beat the hell out of them before calling the cops."

"I'm glad," Brooke asserted firmly. "And I'm very, very glad that you weren't hurt any worse than a broken nose."

"Hey," he protested lightly, "that sucker hurt for a long, long time." His eyes smiled down at her as he traced her lips with his finger. "Are you really glad?"

She nodded. "Very. What happened to Karin?"

"She stayed behind, continuing to chart the various families. I filled out innumerable papers, bribed an outrageous number of Rwandan officials, and finally returned to Cornell with Gloria."

His gaze drifted to the gorilla who had begun rolling down the grassy hill, before climbing up to the top to do it all again. "That was five years ago. We've been together ever since."

His hands suddenly locked behind her head, his thumbs hooking under her jaw to tilt her head back, allowing him to study the depths of her tawny gold eyes. "Marry me, Brooke."

It would be so easy, Brooke mused. All she'd have to do was lean forward the slightest bit and she would feel those firm, wonderful lips against hers again. The idea was so, so tempting.

The piquant aroma of the dark, fertile earth mingled with the sun-warmed grass, while the soft autumn breeze feathered her skin. Somewhere high in the branches of the trees migrating birds were filling the air with their calls. Mother Nature had gone all out, giving them a glorious Indian summer day. It would be so easy to simply quit fighting herself and allow nature to take its course.

"What happened to that scientific observation about us getting to know each other?" Her soft tone faltered slightly as Donovan's hand brushed lightly, teasingly, against her breast.

"We can discover everything we need to know on our honeymoon." His fingers trailed lazily up the inside of her jean-clad thigh.

Brooke closed her eyes to the tender torment. "For a scientific person, that's the most illogical solution I've ever heard."

He pressed her against the blanket, covering her softly pliant body with his own. "I'm damn tired of being a scientist," he warned as his palms skimmed her curves. "Besides, despite all my efforts to convince you of my honorable intentions, I'm coming to the unpleasant conclusion that you don't take me seriously. It's high time I started behaving like a man."

When Donovan's fingers moved to the snap of her jeans, Brooke caught hold of his hands. "Acting like a man doesn't necessarily mean taking whatever you want."

His eyes flamed emerald fire. "I'm not taking anything you don't honestly want to give, Brooke."

As her body instinctively moved against him, Brooke admitted secretly that Donovan's sense of observation was as keen as ever. But during the past weeks she had been forced to consider the idea that she might actually be falling in love with him. If she hadn't always been. And if that were the case, she wasn't about to allow sex to stand in the way of true commitment.

Brooke opened her mouth to demand that Donovan get up when they were both suddenly treated to a shower of colorful autumn leaves. Looking up, they viewed Gloria standing over them. The gorilla's broad teeth flashed yellow in the sunshine as she laughed uproariously at her prank.

"Thank you, Gloria," Brooke said, brushing the leaves from her clothes as she stood up. "You arrived just in the nick of time to save Donovan from another lump on his nose."

Brooke gave Donovan a teasing smile, ignoring his low oath as he rose reluctantly to his feet. "You weren't kidding when you said you were bringing along a chaperon, were you?"

"Remind me to put that beast to bed without her dinner tonight," he muttered. Plucking some russet leaves from her dark hair, he returned Brooke's smile with a reluctant one of his own. "Later," he said quietly.

It could have been a promise. Or a warning. When Brooke took it to be the latter, she tilted her chin defiantly. "No."

Donovan gave her an amused look. "I know you consider it a worn-out cliché," he drawled, "but you sure are cute as the dickens when you get your back up, sweetheart."

"Come on, Gloria," Brooke said, biting down a furious response, "let's you and I go for a walk. I could use some intelligent company for a change." Head held high, she marched off with the still-grinning gorilla toward a stand of colorful oak trees.

Chapter Ten

If Brooke had found their weekend outing a blissful respite from the trials and tribulations of the everyday world, the following week was to prove no different. Donovan began courting her with both words and actions that proved his intentions of wooing and winning her on all levels.

Monday, a paperweight of hand-blown glass arrived at her office via special delivery messenger. The soft blue and gray swirls echoed the hues she had surrounded herself with and each time she looked at it—which was often—Brooke couldn't resist a smile. Donovan, who had never displayed the slightest interest in decorating, had actually remembered the colors of her office. Brooke decided it must be a first.

On Tuesday, President Chambers called Brooke to his office, forcing her to break a lunch date with Donovan. She had no sooner returned to her office when he arrived with a wicker basket. While others might consider a robust Greek salad and hot fudge sundae a strange culinary combination, Brooke couldn't remember when she'd enjoyed a meal more.

Wednesday it rained. Slate-gray clouds banished the usually bright California sunshine and as Brooke drove to the campus, she felt unreasonably out of sorts. She was wading her way through the paperwork covering her desk when the delivery boy showed up with an enormous basket of wildflowers—cheery black-eyed Susans, perky bluebonnets, bright yellow lupines, brilliant, purple-dotted orange Turk's Cap lilies. As the vibrant colors effectively banished the gloomy day, Brooke found the bouquet more enchanting than the most expensive of hothouse blooms.

When the miserable weather continued on Thursday, Brooke found herself waiting to see what Donovan would come up with next. She was not disappointed. The wonderfully huggable, yellow stuffed duck, with his bright orange bill and black button eyes made her smile. When she turned the key under the duck's left wing, a music box offered up a lighthearted rendition of "You are my Sunshine." Brooke laughed delightedly.

Friday brought a carousel horse, cast in hand-painted porcelain. Brooke immediately recognized the brightly painted Mandarin horse as a replica of one from the carousel at the Santa Monica pier. The day after the fraternity mixer where they had met, Brooke and Donovan had joined a group of students seeking to enjoy the last few days of summer at the beach before settling down to their studies. There was something wonderfully romantic about sharing the Philadelphia Toboggan horse with Donovan, his hands over hers on the gleaming brass pole, and from that day on they had laughingly considered "The Carousel Waltz" their song. Brooke was moved that he had remembered.

On Saturday a grinning delivery boy arrived at her apartment and handed her a record album. Unwrapping the bright paper, Brooke was surprised to discover *Patience*, the one Gilbert and Sullivan album she was missing from her collection.

Prithee, pretty maiden, the accompanying note quoted from the record, *will you marry me? Hey, but I'm hopeful, willow willow waly!* To that, Donovan had added a postscript. *No offense, love, but I still contend Gilbert needs Sullivan's music to make his lyrics palatable.*

Donovan's energies were not limited to Brooke alone. It hadn't taken him long to realize that she was an incredibly busy woman, especially with the final budget decisions only a week away. Professors higher up on the collegiate totem pole than he had steadfastly been refused entrance to her office.

He went immediately to work, plying the officious Mrs. Harrigan with a wealth of Irish charm that soon had the woman smiling whenever he approached. Things were looking up, Donovan thought to himself the Saturday after their excursion to the ranch. While Brooke had not repeated her declaration of love, he had become an expert at reading her silences. It was only a matter of time before she'd agree to marry him.

As he dressed for dinner, Donovan did some quick calculations. The Australian Open was in five weeks. While he didn't want to wait that long to make Brooke his wife, the trip would make a dynamite honeymoon. He decided to settle things once and for all this weekend.

"You know," Brooke said as they ate dinner at Stavros's later that evening, "I've really enjoyed the past week."

Donovan frowned as he broke off a piece of fragrant, crusty bread. "You don't have to sound so surprised."

She placed a conciliatory hand on his arm. "I'm sorry. I didn't mean that the way it sounded. It's just that things have been a little hectic since I arrived in Claremont."

"And I haven't helped matters." When she didn't answer immediately, Donovan managed an understanding smile. "Hey, I'm the guy with the stainless-steel feelings, remember? You can be honest with me, Brooke. I can take it."

As Brooke returned Donovan's smile with a soft one of her own, it occurred to her that she had been way off base about his lack of emotions. While he might not display them as easily as some people she knew, the story he had told her about Gloria had been proof that Donovan Kincaid possessed a vast store of feelings.

And she certainly couldn't deny the fact that he'd been a perfect gentleman the past week, courting her with almost an old-world charm that while pleasant, had not pressured her into anything she might not be prepared to give.

"Brooke?"

At his quiet tone, she realized her mind had been wandering. Donovan was waiting for an answer. She struggled to clear her head. "Actually, you're a bit like that old statement about good news and bad news."

Deep furrows marred his tan brow. "I'm not certain I like that."

Brooke was forced to wait as Stavros arrived to take away the empty soup bowls. She smiled her thanks as he deposited a delicious-looking lamb stew in front of her.

"This is absolutely marvelous," she professed enthusiastically, taking a taste of the stew served over fried manestra. The pasta was the size of cantaloupe seeds. She eyed Donovan's stuffed eggplant covetously. "Of course yours looks great, too. That's the problem with eating here. Everything Stavros cooks is so terrific, I can never make up my mind. Want to trade bites?"

Donovan put his fork down. "I want to know what you meant by that good news, bad news crack."

Brooke's eyes widened at his suddenly gritty tone. "My, aren't we touchy tonight?"

"Enforced celibacy tends to do that to a man," he muttered.

Brooke lowered her own fork to the table as well with a soft, resigned sigh. "We agreed," she reminded him.

"*You* agreed," Donovan pointed out. "I thought it was a dumb idea. I still do."

"There's more to a relationship than sex."

"Don't you think I know that?" he countered on a tight flare of temper. "I'm the one who came up with the idea of us getting to know each other better in the first place."

"That was," Brooke admitted with a slight dip of her head, "a very good plan."

"Of course it was. But I still can't see what the hell it has to do with you refusing to make love with me." When Brooke remained silent, he leaned toward her, his fingers gripping her leg under the table.

"You can lie your head off if you want, Brooke, but if Gloria hadn't been out at the ranch last weekend, we would have made love. Hell," he tacked on in a husky voice, "we'd probably still be there, lying under the stars."

His fingers stroked her thigh. "I've always loved the way your skin looks in the moonlight. Do you have any idea how hard it's been for me to keep my hands off you all week? When all I can think about is touching you. Tasting you. Loving you."

Brooke closed her eyes against the flood of desire surging through her veins. "Don't do this," she whispered.

"You're the one who set the rules, sweetheart," Donovan taunted softly. "Don't blame me if I find them too restrictive to play by."

Amber eyes flew open as she fixed him with a warning look. "This isn't a game, Donovan."

"I know."

For a long, tense moment they simply stared at each other, each waiting for the other to back down. Just when Brooke's nerves were at the breaking point, Stavros appeared at their table.

"Something wrong with the dinner?" he asked, taking in the barely touched food.

"Nothing at all," Donovan assured him without taking his eyes from Brooke's face. "Everything's excellent. As usual."

The Greek nodded his satisfaction. "Of course it is. So eat while it's still hot," he instructed. "And save the arguing for later—it's bad for business."

His teeth flashed under the shaggy mustache. "My customers come here for Stavros's magnificent food in order to forget their problems. Your two sour faces will remind them that they are unhappy. That idea will give them stomachaches and they will not be able to eat. Stavros will go bankrupt, be forced to close the restaurant and return home with his Anna to Athens in disgrace. A failure."

The huge Greek shrugged expansively, stretching out his arms. "How could such nice people live with your consciences, knowing that you had done such a sad and terrible thing to one of your best friends?''

Brooke laughed as she shook her head. ''I'm beginning to understand the *kamaki*.''

Stavros's answering smile was broad and his black eyes twinkled merrily. ''Of course you are.'' He pointed to her plate. ''Now eat, before it gets cold.'' With that he strode away, leaving them alone again.

''Bossy bastard,'' Donovan mumbled.

''Is that any way to talk about your best friend?''

''Stavros is that,'' Donovan agreed reluctantly as he scooped a forkful of the ground meat mixture from the eggplant. ''He actually offered to lend me the money to replace Gloria's television.''

Brooke's fork had been on the way to her mouth, but at Donovan's casual statement she lowered it once again to the table. Who would have suspected that Stavros was the answer to Donovan's funding problem? Over the past weeks Brooke had been growing increasingly nervous, waiting for Donovan's reaction when he discovered she had vetoed his request for a new television. But if he could get the money elsewhere, there would be no reason for him to be angry at her for denying him the funds. Brooke had to restrain herself from jumping up from the table and hugging the ebullient old Greek.

''What did you say?'' She struggled to keep the excitement from her voice.

Donovan shrugged. ''Same thing I told Alex and Serena when they offered,'' he replied. ''I turned him down.''

Brooke's hands turned to ice. ''Why on earth would you do that?''

''It's the principle of the thing.''

''Principle?''

"Hell, Brooke, if it were merely the money, I'd buy the damn television myself. While my salary is admittedly nothing to shout about, I've managed to put away some money."

"I don't understand," she said quietly. She had almost forgotten how intransigent Donovan could be when he set his mind to something. Damned stubborn Irishman. Why was he determined to make it so difficult?

Donovan wondered how they had jumped from discussing their love life to the topic of his work. Mindful of Brooke's accusation that he had neglected her for his research, he had struggled not to repeat past mistakes. He had refrained from talking about his work unless asked, and despite the fact that it was now Gloria who was complaining about being neglected, he had adjusted his schedule to Brooke's.

It hadn't been easy balancing his professional life with his personal one—on more than one occasion Donovan had felt as if he was walking a high wire without a net. But it had been worth it. Brooke had been worth it.

He frowned as he struggled to put his thoughts into words she might understand. "It's not a simple matter of money," he repeated slowly. "If I'm to succeed in my research, Brooke, I need to feel the college is behind me, one hundred percent."

Donovan's words chilled Brooke's blood. "Of course they are," she insisted.

"Perhaps. Perhaps not. We'll find out for sure when the board of regents meets Monday morning, won't we?"

It took a vast effort, but Brooke won the battle against the guilty flush that threatened to darken her cheeks. "I suppose we will," she murmured noncommittally.

"The money is only a symbol, Brooke," he stressed. "A sign that they support my work, believe in it."

Brooke couldn't let his veiled accusation pass. "Don't you think everyone feels that way?" she argued. "But if it were that simple, Donovan, if the college gave every professor what he or she was asking for, we'd end up with Professor Stevenson building atomic bombs in the chemistry labs, while General Osborne was busy creating Star Wars weaponry in the physics department.

"Not to mention Bev Ormsbee conducting her psychology lectures atop a mountain in Nepal, while her class studied biofeedback from some guru, and your own brother-in-law taking his students on a tour of the Middle East during spring break."

Donovan arched a dark brow. "Alex is actually requesting funds for a vacation jaunt?"

Brooke's soft sigh of aggravation blew her bangs off her forehead. She couldn't remember a time when she had behaved so irresponsibly. "I shouldn't have told you that."

"Alex never said anything," Donovan mused, taking a sip of his wine. The retsina possessed a rich pine resin that complemented the Greek fare.

"I shouldn't have, either. The proposals are supposed to be confidential."

He gave her a reassuring smile. "Don't worry, Brooke, I won't let your secret out."

Knowing that she could indeed trust him made Brooke feel slightly better. Still, she couldn't banish a lingering sense of self-irritation.

"If I were you," Donovan advised, "I'd get busy on that lamb stew before Stavros returns with another lecture."

Knowing Donovan's prediction to be accurate, Brooke put the nagging little problem from her mind and turned her attention to Stavros's excellent cooking.

"You never did tell me what you meant by the fact that I was good news and bad news," Donovan reminded Brooke as his MG idled outside her apartment building.

"It's a bit complicated," she hedged.

He immediately leaned forward, twisting the key to turn off the ignition. "I've all the time in the world."

In deference to the cool, autumn night temperatures, he had put up the rag top on the MG. The close confines of the sports car were unnervingly intimate and the way Donovan was looking at her, his green eyes warming her face, did not help matters.

"Did I thank you for this latest gift?" she asked, nervously twisting the mirrored end of the brass kaleidoscope he had given her at dinner.

"You did. Three times, as a matter of fact. And I told you those bright colors remind me of how I feel when we make love.... Are you by any chance stalling?"

"I suppose I am," she answered on a reluctant sigh. When she met his smiling gaze, Brooke's expression was inordinately solemn. "There are times when I think you're the best thing that ever happened to me," she admitted quietly.

He leaned toward her, stretching his arm along the back of her seat. "Why do I hear a *but* in that declaration?"

He had effectively blocked any means of escape, but Brooke couldn't have moved away had she wanted to. His intimate gaze, abetted by her own tumultuous feelings, was effectively holding her hostage.

"Because I'm afraid that I'll fall in love with you all over again."

He trailed a finger down her cheek. "Would that be so terrible?"

"I don't know." She closed her eyes against his tender touch as his finger traced the line of her jaw. "You have to understand, Donovan, I've worked hard to get where I am. I make my living in a field where problems are solved in a rational, mathematical way. I'm not accustomed to feeling this way."

As he caressed the soft skin of her throat, Donovan could feel Brooke's pulse increase under his touch. The idea that she wanted him, loved him, made control difficult, but he understood on some deep inner level that this could well be one of the most important conversations of his life.

"What way?"

Her eyes were swimming with moisture as she met his gently coaxing gaze. "Out of control. Confused. I can't help wondering if I'm only responding to past memories, seeking some small comfort because my work here is so difficult."

He tried not to smile at her earnest tone, recalling his own sleepless nights as he had struggled with much the same worries.

"Something very strange seems to have happened here," he said quietly, drawing her into a comforting embrace. "It appears we've managed to swap personalities."

"What do you mean?" she mumbled into his jacket as she wrapped her arms around him.

When he pressed his lips against the top of her head, Brooke could feel his smile against her hair. "Although I'm supposed to be the scientist, I'm perfectly willing to admit that I love you without any rational reason for such an occurrence.''

He brushed the hair back from her face, allowing his lips to brush her temple. ''While you, whose impetuosity I used to find undeniably exciting and even a little unsettling from time to time, insist on dissecting your emotions to death.''

She lifted her head to look at him curiously. ''I seem to recall you saying that I needed to curb my impulsive tendencies.''

''I probably did say something dumb like that. All I can offer in my defense is that it took me a while to realize a good thing when I had it.''

His expression turned intensely serious. ''I'd like nothing more than to be able to admit that after we broke up, I spent these past years regretting the fact that I was fool enough to let you get away.''

''But you didn't,'' she guessed accurately.

''No, I didn't. Instead I buried myself even deeper in my work. To tell you the truth, I didn't realize how dark and narrow my life had become until just lately.'' His green eyes swept over her face. ''Do you believe in fate?''

Brooke's mouth went suddenly dry. ''I think so,'' she whispered. ''At least I used to.''

Donovan's lips curved in a smile, but his gaze remained unnervingly sober. ''I never did,'' he said in a low gravelly voice. ''But ever since your return to Claremont, I've begun to wonder.''

''Oh, Donovan,'' Brooke said on a soft rippling sigh, ''I don't know what to think.''

It wouldn't be difficult, Donovan calculated as he stroked soothing circles on her back. A single kiss, perhaps two, some softly spoken words and he could be sharing Brooke's bed tonight. By her own admission she was exhausted, confused and unsettled by all the changes in her life. Why shouldn't he be the one to bring her temporary respite from her problems?

The key word was *temporary*, Donovan allowed reluctantly. While he knew Brooke would succumb to his seduction techniques tonight, there was a good chance she'd find herself regretting such impulsive behavior in the morning. He was beginning to understand her perhaps better than she did herself. Everything thus far indicated that she would view her brief slip as weakness. Donovan didn't want to win that way.

There was a vulnerability in her distressed gaze that had Donovan wanting Brooke more than he ever had. That same vulnerability was what would keep him from making love to her until she was very sure of her own mind. When Brooke came to him, and he had no doubt that she would, he wanted her to come on her own terms. Able to admit her love openly, without hesitation.

He put a finger under her chin, lifting her downcast face to his. "Then don't think," he advised. "Why don't you try following your feelings, instead?"

"You make it sound so easy," she protested.

"I love you, Brooke," he said firmly. "And I want to marry you."

She could feel the moisture welling up behind her lids and swore she wouldn't cry. "Donovan, please...."

When she would have turned away, his fingers tightened. "I love you," he repeated firmly. "But I'm not talented enough to pen sonnets comparing your beauty to a summer's day and I can't afford to buy you the diamonds and sapphires you deserve."

When he appeared convinced that she would allow him his say, Donovan released Brooke, taking her hand in his. "When we're apart, I think up all these wonderful, romantic things to say, but as soon as I'm around you, I find myself turning into a tongue-tied adolescent."

He ran his thumb lightly over her knuckles. "That's one of the reasons I enjoy making love to you. Besides the obvious one," he added with a crooked grin. "It's a way to show you how I feel. How precious you are to me."

The small pulse of excitement that had been beating deep inside her all day had increased exponentially during his fervently issued speech.

"For someone who's supposed to be so bad with words, you're certainly saying all the right things tonight."

"I'm sure as hell trying." He bent his head, brushing his lips against hers.

Brooke returned the kiss with equal lightness. "Damn you," she complained. "You could always weaken my defenses. Despite your alleged lack of romantic gestures."

"Is that what I'm doing?" he asked, trailing his lips down her throat.

Irresistible. There was a force about Donovan Kincaid that was impossible to resist, even if she had wanted to. Which Brooke was not so certain that she did.

"Aren't you?" She thrust her fingers through his hair, drawing his lips back to hers.

Donovan took her mouth with infinite care. It had been a long, lonely week of cold showers and sleepless nights. He had every intention of savoring this moment.

Brooke trembled as Donovan traced her lips with the tip of his tongue. Tasting, teasing, skimming over her skin with a touch so light, so delicate, she might have thought she imagined it.

"I've missed you," he murmured. "I've missed making love with you. I've missed going to sleep with my arms around you, seeing your face first thing when I wake up in the morning. I've missed your smile, your laughter, the way your hands feel on my flesh.... I've missed everything about you, Brooke." As he caressed her breast, Brooke felt a spark leap under his touch.

"Oh, more," she insisted, pressing her hands against the back of his head.

"More," he agreed on a hot rush of breath.

But even as Brooke prepared herself for the storm she had come to expect from Donovan, he surprised her. His teeth captured her bottom lip, nipping and tugging until he had created a slow, almost painful echo deep inside her. A low moan escaped her throat.

Brooke's mouth clung to his, surrendering to the seduction of his tongue, the warmth of his breath, the scorching fire of possession that passed between them. The kiss went on and on, growing more and more powerful, the passion it incited escalating until the air practically crackled around them in the cramped interior of the sports car.

Despite the fact that his intentions had been honorable when he had begun to kiss Brooke, Donovan found himself contemplating the logistics of taking her here. Now. The tawdriness of that idea, combined with his determination to do things right this time, had him reluctantly lifting his head to break the heated contact.

Brooke could only stare as Donovan leaned his head back against the seat and closed his eyes. "Talk about your trips back in time. I feel just like some oversexed, randy teenager. I can't remember the last time I attempted to make love to a woman in a car.''

With Donovan's eyes closed, Brooke felt free to study him. Now that he had pointed it out, she could see where his nose had been broken. Otherwise, he was certainly no slouch in the looks department.

In the beginning, she had missed his beard. But she had come to the conclusion that all that chestnut facial hair had done was detract from Donovan's firm, square jaw. As her gaze moved to his shuttered eyes, Brooke found herself once again reflecting on Mother Nature's inequities. It was simply not fair that a man should be given such thick, curly eyelashes.

Her mind conjured up another day, long ago, when those lashes had rested on his cheeks. But that day, his face had been white with pain. Pain he had tried his best to conceal.

"I would have thought that our Christmas Eve fiasco broke you of the habit of trying to do anything remotely physical in this sardine can."

Donovan smiled at the long-ago memory. "That fateful afternoon we went skiing at Big Bear. If I recall correctly, we were on the way back here when I couldn't stand it any longer and pulled off the road to park."

"And in your enthusiasm, you got caught up on the gear shift and broke your ankle."

When Donovan opened his eyes, they were smiling at her. "You have to admit, it was undoubtedly the most interesting case the ski patrol had all day."

Brooke returned his reminiscent smile. "They couldn't stop laughing. Although your lovemaking techniques demonstrated as much flair as you showed all day on the slopes."

He arched a challenging brow. "Are you accusing me of being a bad skier?"

"Not at all. You were, without a doubt, the sexiest man on the bunny slope."

"Why don't you sweet-talk me some more," Donovan suggested dryly. "Since I seem to remember being the only male over the age of six on the beginners' trail that afternoon."

Brooke laughed. "I'm amazed that you remembered that little detail."

His expression suddenly sobered. "Over the past few weeks I've discovered that I remember everything about those days, Brooke. Including the fact that you felt sorry enough for me to give me my Christmas present a few hours early."

Brooke felt the color rush into her cheeks at the memory of their lovemaking that evening. The doctor had warned her that the pain medication would probably make Donovan sleep right through Christmas. His diagnosis couldn't have been more wrong.

"How many times did we make love that night?" Donovan mused aloud.

"I don't remember," Brooke lied softly.

"I think we set a record. But of course we had a lot to celebrate."

"That was the week you got accepted into graduate school at Cornell." At the time, Brooke had foolishly believed she would be going to New York with him.

"True, but that's not what I was talking about. It was the day I realized for the first time that I was in love with you."

"Oh." Her heart skipped a beat.

"Oh," he mimicked, not unkindly. "What are you doing tomorrow?"

"Spending the day with you?"

He bent down, giving her a quick, hard kiss on the lips. The brief flare ended all too soon. "Got it on the first try."

"Is Gloria coming along?"

Donovan grinned as he ruffled her hair. "I think it might be a bit difficult to sneak her into the Montgomery Art Gallery, don't you?"

"We're going to the exhibit?"

"We are if you still like Fairfield Porter."

Brooke shook her head with honest admiration. "I didn't think you were listening when I used to talk about how much I admired his work."

Donovan shrugged as he opened his car door. "I didn't think I was, either," he admitted. "I guess I just absorbed it all on some subconscious level. The mind's funny that way. You'd be surprised what Gloria actually seems to remember about being in the bush."

Brooke experienced a rush of something that felt a great deal like love as she watched Donovan come around the front of the car. He appeared to be trying so hard. The least she could do would be to meet him halfway.

Brooke didn't offer a word of protest as Donovan took her hand as they walked into her apartment building. She allowed her body to lean into his, she permitted her lips to melt enticingly against his mouth as she gave herself up to the sheer pleasure of his good-night kiss.

But when Donovan might have reinitiated his campaign to make love to her, he retreated, promising to see her again in a few hours.

As she prepared for bed, Brooke found herself wishing that he had not taken her refusal quite so literally.

Chapter Eleven

The insistent ringing of the doorbell eventually filtered its way into Brooke's unconscious mind. Casting a quick disbelieving glance at her clock radio, she pulled the flower-sprigged sheets over her head and closed her eyes tight. But whoever was out there was obviously not going to go away. Muttering an oath, Brooke crawled from the warmth of the bed, stumbling into the other room.

Peering through the viewer in the center of the door, she glimpsed Donovan, stepping from foot to foot as he waited impatiently for her to open the door.

"What are you doing here?" she demanded, dragging her thick, sleep-tousled hair back from her face with an impatient gesture.

"Good morning to you, too," Donovan answered cheerily as he entered her apartment. "I've brought you breakfast."

"I don't eat breakfast."

"And the Sunday L.A. *Times*."

"I never read anything before noon on Sunday."

He waved the white bag under her nose, allowing a delicious, enticing scent to waft up. "I even brought coffee," he coaxed.

"Bingo. You just said the magic word." Brooke shut the door. "Go on into the kitchen," she instructed. "I'll get dressed and be right in."

Donovan's appreciative gaze slid down her royal-blue silk nightshirt. "You certainly don't have to change on my account," he drawled. "Personally, I prefer the scenery precisely the way it is."

"Your breakfast is leaking." Brooke pointed out the dark stain spreading across the bottom of the bag. With that she turned to leave the room.

As she walked away, Donovan debated whether or not she was wearing anything under that brief nightshirt and decided that she wasn't. He cursed silently, wondering how much longer he could maintain his distance.

After dressing, Brooke found Donovan out on her terrace, his feet propped up on the wrought-iron railing as he perused the sports page.

"I like that outfit," he said, his bright eyes paying compliments as they took in the cream-colored angora sweater and lightweight wool slacks.

"Generous words from a man who drags me out of bed at the crack of dawn," she retorted, settling into a chair with an annoyed flounce.

"Eight o'clock is not exactly the crack of dawn, Brooke," Donovan argued as he handed her a cup of coffee.

She took a sip of the steaming hot brew, receiving a satisfying jolt as the caffeine entered her bloodstream. "It is on Sunday."

"That's not very scientific," he complained. "The day of the week doesn't have anything to do with when the sun comes up."

"I thought you were going to stop acting like a scientist."

The newspaper fluttered unnoticed to the concrete. "You're right, I was. Thanks for reminding me."

Donovan lowered his feet, put his hands on her shoulders and took her mouth before Brooke had time to realize that he had taken her words as a direct challenge.

There was no slow seduction, no gentle teasing. This time the desire sprang full-blown, whirling them quickly into passion. If Brooke was shocked by the strength of Donovan's mouth as he crushed her lips with ruthless kisses, she was even more stunned by her instantaneous response. She had no choice but to hang on for dear life as his kisses took her deeper and deeper into the swirling vortex of dark desire.

Control began slipping away. Donovan's body, which he had managed to force into reluctant submission, stirred as Brooke's mouth clung desperately to his. Slowly, reluctantly, he backed away from temptation.

Brooke's eyes, as they looked up at him, were still confused and softly clouded. "I spilled coffee on you," she said finally.

Donovan followed her gaze to his thigh, where a damp stain darkened the tan corduroy. "Don't worry about it, it'll sponge out." Laugh lines crinkled outward from his smiling eyes. "Although a few inches higher and you could have done in our chances for a large family."

His teasing words, coming so soon after that savage kiss, stirred a deeply hidden primitive desire. As old as time itself, it was the ache of a woman for her mate. Needs, physical and emotional, surged through her.

Brooke struggled to keep her tone composed as she rose from the white wrought-iron chair. "I'll get a towel." As she escaped the terrace, she didn't see the slow, satisfied smile curving Donovan's lips.

Alone in the kitchen, Brooke rested her forehead against the cool enamel of the refrigerator. What on earth had made her think she could keep things on a casual, platonic level with Donovan Kincaid? She was truly deceiving herself.

And she was every bit as guilty as Donovan for the fact that things kept getting out of hand. From now on, she vowed, quickly grabbing a towel and dampening it, she was going to make certain that she didn't offer the man any more encouragement.

Donovan grinned up at her as she returned to the terrace. "Want me to take these off?" he asked helpfully, his hands moving to his belt buckle.

"That won't be necessary." She thrust the towel down at him. "Here."

"Why don't you sponge it off?" he suggested amiably. "You're probably much better at it than I am."

"Good try, but I'm sure you can handle a little coffee stain yourself, Donovan."

He sighed as he accepted the towel and began wiping at the stain. As the gesture pulled the corduroy taut against his hips, Brooke found her unruly mind creating stimulating images. She threw herself back into the chair and picked up the first piece of newspaper her hand touched.

"All done," Donovan announced a bit later. He tossed the towel onto the table. "I didn't know you liked bass fishing."

"I don't." Brooke refused to look up at him.

"But you find it interesting?"

"I've never found the idea of putting hooks through squiggling worms in order to capture a slippery, slimy fish remotely interesting," she returned. "So if you have that in mind for one of our little get-acquainted outings, Donovan, I think I'll pass, if it's all the same to you."

"Hey, I'm not that wild about fishing, either," he protested. "I've never quite had the patience for it. Although a lot can be said for the scenery. Do you remember the time we went out to Lake Arrowhead and—"

"Did you bring up fishing for any particular reason? Or is this just another stroll down memory lane?" She shot him an irritated glance over the top of the newspaper.

His eyes met hers, bright and curious. "I just wondered why you were reading the outdoors page. It's all about bass fishing today."

Brooke stared down at the newspaper she had been pretending to read, forcing her eyes to focus on the swimming black print.

"Actually, I was interested in the financial aspects of bass fishing."

"Financial?"

Her eyes raced down the page, drinking in paragraphs of text at a time. "Financial," she repeated, more firmly this time. "It appears that they have contests."

"Bass?"

"Fishermen," she corrected impatiently. "It says here that a good fisherman can win over a hundred thousand a year in prize money."

"That's a lot of worms."

"It's also a great deal of money. For fishing."

"So it is," Donovan agreed thoughtfully. "Would that matter to you, Brooke?"

"Matter?"

"Money," he repeated. "It hasn't escaped my notice that those lacy underthings you've taken to wearing definitely don't come from Kmart. Could you possibly fall in love with a man who didn't bring in a six-figure income?"

Brooke's gaze was steady as her eyes met his. "I think," she said slowly, "I already have."

Before giving him a chance to respond, she cast a glance down at the slim gold watch circling her wrist. "Heavens, look at the time," she said on a rush of words. "We'd better get going before the gallery is packed with people."

"Brooke—"

"No," she insisted almost desperately, "not now."

From her breathless tone, Donovan realized that Brooke had not intended to offer such an admission. The words had come spontaneously in a way that reminded him of the young student he had once loved. She had allowed her true feelings to surface. Just a little more time, he told himself, counseling patience. He'd made it this far. Surely he could survive a few more hours.

"Later."

His eyes were so dark, so intense, it was difficult to believe that the gentle fingertips touching her cheek belonged to the same man. Brooke closed her eyes on a quiet, accepting sigh.

"Yes."

They were extremely careful for the rest of the morning. As if by unspoken agreement, both seemed determined to keep things casual. For the time being. But neither Brooke nor Donovan could entirely banish the sense of anticipation that followed close on their footsteps, reminding them of all they had left unsaid.

Since Brooke had dragged them from her apartment long before the exhibit was scheduled to open, they passed the time visiting Gloria. When Brooke saw the way the television picture was rolling dangerously, the color fading to black and white with increasing regularity, she found herself dreading tomorrow morning when the board was scheduled to announce the grant recipients.

Would Donovan still want anything to do with her when he discovered that she'd vetoed two-thirds of his proposal? She shook her head as they walked the few short blocks to the Montgomery Gallery, refusing to allow anything, especially thoughts of work, to ruin this day.

They wandered the gallery, stopping long enough in front of each exhibit to allow Brooke to explain something about the painter's style of realism.

"Just look at that," Brooke said almost reverently as she stood before one painting brimming with joyous color. "Isn't it incredible?"

"Incredible," Donovan murmured.

To his admittedly undiscerning eye, "Island Farmhouse" was a basically simple, rather old-fashioned picture. But he was definitely enjoying Brooke's excitement with the exhibit. Her eyes gleamed gold in her enthusiasm, reminiscent of how they appeared when she was aroused. Thinking of how long it had been since they had made love, Donovan was forced to stifle an inward groan of frustration.

"Look at those supple brush strokes," she said, her gaze still directed toward the painting. "I wish I were talented."

He ran his hand down her arm. "I think you are."

"That's not what my Art 101 professor said when I humiliated myself for eleven long weeks in his classroom. Do you want to know a secret?" she asked with a half smile as she looked up at him. "One I've never told a single solitary soul?"

"I want to know all your secrets, Brooke. That's what this getting-to-know-you routine has been about, remember?"

Brooke was shaken by the intensity in Donovan's eyes. What had begun as a casual, safe conversation had suddenly escalated, taking on deeper meaning. She knew that if she left with Donovan right now, they'd be making love before they got to her bedroom. The idea was undeniably exciting. Brooke tried to remind herself that she'd already had two strikes in the game of love. She wasn't certain she was strong enough to survive a third.

"Brooke?"

Desperately, hurriedly, she gathered her scattered thoughts. "When I was growing up, I dreamed of being a great artist," she related with a slight self-deprecating smile. "You've no idea how discouraging it is to discover that Gloria probably has more artistic talent in her little finger than I do in my entire body."

Donovan laced their fingers together, his thumb brushing her palm. "Don't worry about it, love. Your talents lie in an entirely different area altogether."

His words, murmured next to her ear, along with the tantalizing caress, caused a feeling of arousal to rush through her. "Isn't this exhilarating," Brooke declared brightly, pulling him in the direction of a brilliantly crisp work entitled "Ice Storm."

"I've certainly always thought so," he agreed, running his palm down the back of her leg.

"Stop that," Brooke hissed, jerking away from him. "I was referring to the exhibit."

"What makes you think I wasn't?" he asked, his wide green eyes appearing absolutely guileless.

"Wretch," Brooke muttered, returning her attention to the painting. "This has always been one of my favorite Fairfield Porter works."

"Why?" Hearing the emotion in her tone, Donovan studied the painting more intently. To his surprise he felt as if he was actually breathing in the icy air, hearing the crunch of the snow underfoot.

"He painted it during a winter he spent at Amherst," Brooke informed him quietly. "It was hanging in a San Francisco museum that first year you were at Cornell. I used to drive up from Menlo Park on the weekend just to look at it."

For the second time in his life, Donovan wished he were a wealthy man. The first time had been when he had been forced to accept the idea that if he asked Brooke to accompany him to Cornell, he never would've been able to support her in the style to which she had become accustomed. As Brooke's attention remained riveted on the painting, Donovan wished he possessed the funds to purchase it for her on the spot.

"You must have really liked it a lot to spend your weekends driving back and forth between Menlo Park and the city."

"It wasn't that," she murmured, her eyes still directed toward the icy scene. "I'd look at it and wonder if that's how things were for you."

"It was similar." Donovan, who had never really taken the time to notice such things, now recalled that the winter sky over Ithaca had been a cold, white, almost unearthly shade. Porter, Donovan acknowledged, had captured it perfectly.

"I hadn't realized you thought of me in those days."

Brooke warily lifted her gaze, shaken when she found everything she was feeling in Donovan's eyes. Desire, frustration, regret. They were all there.

"I never stopped thinking about you."

Before Donovan could respond to that statement, Brooke had walked on, talking rapidly, expounding on the emergence of the painter as he moved from works subdued in color and impressionist in handling to a looser, broader explosion of color that dazzled the senses.

"Do you really want to hang around here any longer?" he asked after they'd completed their tour of the gallery.

The shortbread cookie stopped on the way to Brooke's mouth. "Not if you're ready to leave." She slowly lowered her cup of fruit punch to the table.

"I am," he admitted. "Unless you want to socialize."

Brooke almost laughed at that. Besides the paintings, she had only been aware of Donovan's presence in the gallery. The other gallery patrons had been no more than an indistinct blur.

"Let's go," she said, linking her arm through his.

As they walked out into the mellow October air, Brooke admitted to herself for the first time that she was going to marry Donovan Kincaid. A slow, secret smile curved her lips as she imagined his response.

"You know," Donovan said thoughtfully as they entered Brooke's apartment, "I'm getting to like this place."

Brooke cast a quick glance around her living room. "It's not so bad, I suppose," she murmured. "For a nun's cell."

Donovan had the good grace to grimace. "Did I really call it that?"

Brooke folded her arms. "You certainly did."

His eyes made a slow, deliberate study of the room. While he was no expert on decorating, he realized that the room reflected its owner. Serene, elegant, with an unmistakable style all its own. A veritable palette of pastels had been washed over the interior of the apartment—the walls were a light blue, the grayish white Mexican tile floor covered with Oriental rugs in soft blues and rose that reminded him of sunrise. The tall ceramic vases held lilies and delphinium, the floral arrangements soft drifts of color that almost appeared to have washed off one of the Monet landscapes hanging on the wall. At first glance, one received a feeling of peace, quiet.

But on closer observation, Donovan noticed the bright accents of color—a glossy red candle in the shape of a plump apple, a bright blue ceramic bowl, a sunshine-yellow quilt tossed with careful casualness over the arm of a pewter-gray wing chair. The unexpected colors echoed the passion that ran just beneath Brooke's cool exterior. He wondered idly how many individuals had taken time to discover those flashes of emotion.

"Well?"

"It's you," he said slowly.

A smile teased at the corners of her mouth. "Neat."

"No. Well, that, too," he said, wondering how she managed to keep things so tidy when her days were every bit as full as his. Donovan decided that such behavior must be a talent. Like the ability to sing on key. Or tap-dance. Whatever, he was decidedly lacking in that particular gift.

"Actually, I was thinking how your apartment was full of surprises. Like some serene, but scintillatingly sensual lady I happen to know."

Brooke's smile moved upward to her eyes. "Feel like another surprise?" she asked mildly.

She was so damned lovely. Her almond eyes shone with golden lights, a soft flush darkened her cheeks, her hair gleamed like burnished silk. Donovan could feel the pull, that slow, unmistakably erotic pull. He slipped his hands into his pockets to keep from crossing the room and dragging her down onto one of those plush Oriental rugs.

"I've always been a sucker for surprises." He prided himself on his control when his voice remained as nonchalant as Brooke's.

Her next words, while not entirely unexpected, struck him like a bolt of lightning. "I love you, Donovan Kincaid. I think I've always loved you. And I want to marry you. As soon as the state of California allows." As she took a deep breath, Brooke saw his shoulders tense.

Donovan was stunned by the emotions flooding through him. He had always expected to feel a rush of self-satisfaction when she finally accepted his proposal. But as often as he had thought of this moment, fantasized about it, he had never imagined the warmth, the gratitude, the almost overwhelming relief he would experience. His mind was crowded with words, but the feelings hammering away inside him made speech impossible.

A seductive smile teased at her lips as Brooke crossed the room to stand in front of him. Framing his face with her hands, she coaxed his mouth down to hers.

"I love you," she whispered, her breath warm on his skin as her lips brushed against his. "Love you." She pressed a kiss against his jaw. "Love you."

Had there ever been such exciting words? Donovan's fingers tangled in her hair as he recaptured her mouth. Passion built in him as the kiss went deeper and deeper, sweeping them both into a world of swirling smoke and blazing fire.

Brooke's fingers were nimble, unbuttoning his shirt as she kept her mouth fused to his. The oxford cloth fluttered unheeded to the floor. Her hands skimmed over his shoulders, her fingers tracing the hard, smooth line of muscles in his upper back, teasing, tantalizing, never remaining still.

When Donovan would have lifted her in his arms, intent on carrying her into the bedroom, Brooke shook her head. "Now," she whispered. "I need you now."

He needed no further invitation. Passion scorched his brain as he pulled her into his arms and together they slid to the floor. When he slipped his hands under her cream sweater to caress her breasts, he found the nipples already taut. With one swift, deft motion, he tugged the sweater over Brooke's head and dropped it uncaringly beside his shirt.

"Do you know what it does to me to know that I can do this to you?" he asked huskily, pushing aside the creamy lace of Brooke's bra to bury his mouth in the soft yielding flesh. "Do you have any idea how exciting it is to know that with just my hands, my lips, I can make you mine? All mine?"

"Yours," Brooke agreed on a gasp. A moment later, with a speed that left him stunned, she was lying across his chest, her lips nibbling at his love-moist skin. "And you're mine."

As her mouth roamed lazily over Donovan's chest, Brooke could feel the thunderous beat of his heart under her lips. Her tongue cut a wet swathe through the arrowing of dark hair, moving steadily downward, over his rib cage, across his taut stomach, wrenching moans from deep within him as she continued her sensual journey.

While their lovemaking had always been fulfilling, exciting, Brooke had always allowed Donovan the more aggressive role. She had never played the seductress before. But now, as she tortured him with teasing, tantalizing caresses, Brooke was giddy with a sense of power like nothing she had ever known.

"All mine," she said on a throaty laugh as she toyed with the buckle of his belt.

"My God, Brooke," Donovan groaned on a harsh, ragged breath as she slid the denim down his hips, "you're enough to drive a man mad."

As her lips nibbled a path back up his legs, stopping briefly at his thighs, Donovan couldn't remember wanting anyone as much as he did Brooke at this moment. He struggled desperately to maintain hold of some slender thread of control.

Brooke lifted her head, her brilliant eyes feverish with shared desire. It was coming as a surprise that passion laced with love surpassed anything she had ever known. It had a power, a force, a glory all its own.

Abruptly she pressed her slender body against the length of his, crushing his mouth in a moist open-mouthed kiss. "Let's be mad," she begged, her hands racing over him. Hurriedly. Desperately. "Oh, yes, my darling. Let's be mad together."

The pace quickened as Donovan's hands tore at the remainder of Brooke's clothing. Her wool slacks landed on a chair across the room, bits of lace and silk were strewn heedlessly across the floor. Madness had them in its grasp, pulling them deeper and deeper and deeper into a steamy place where logic gave way to passion. Where reason was unknown. And insanity reigned supreme.

Their hands explored each other ruthlessly, exploiting previously undiscovered flash points of pleasure; their mouths were greedy in their need to taste, to savor. Brooke was lying full length on him, her long slender legs entangled with his, the heat of her body like nothing Donovan had ever known. It seeped into him, scorching his skin, melting his bones.

How strong he was. How hard. Brooke's hands slid down his sides, lingering at his hips just long enough to evoke a husky moan. His skin was burning hot, slick, fragrant with a male musk that made her head spin, her body throb. The room grew warmer, the air thicker. Swirling mists clouded her brain.

Just when Brooke was certain that she was no longer capable of breathing, Donovan's long fingers grasped her hips. He arched his back and plunged inside her, taking her fully, completely.

Brooke's muffled cry of wonder broke off as he surged upward, again and again, driving her further and further into the shimmering golden mists. Her fingernails dug into his shoulders as she clung to him, having no choice but to follow him to a place where the light was resplendent, growing more incandescent still until it was blinding in its intensity. When she closed her eyes to escape its brilliant glare, Brooke found the effort fruitless; behind her lids phosphorescent shooting stars were exploding on a background of black velvet.

Brooke's mind was swirling with thoughts of Donovan as the final flash overtook her. Then there was only a black, swirling darkness.

Chapter Twelve

It was the sparkling sunshine scent of her hair, splayed over his chest, that finally coaxed his mind back to reality. Donovan played with the silken strands, twisting them around his hands.

"You are so lovely it takes my breath away."

Riding on soft waves of contentment, Brooke didn't bother to open her eyes. "Mmm. Who says you don't know how to sweet-talk a woman?" she murmured, pressing her lips against his chest.

He nibbled playfully on her ear. "It's certainly never been my forte, you must bring out the romantic in me."

Her lashes fluttered open as she twined her arms around his neck. "I love romance." Her mouth found his. "And I love you." Brooke could hardly believe how easily the words came. Or how good they made her feel.

His light kisses moved to her jaw. "It's about time. Although I suppose I should be grateful for small favors. You did manage to save me a fortune these past few weeks."

Hers. He was all hers, Brooke thought giddily as she pressed her lips against his shoulder. "Really? How did I do that?"

Donovan cupped the back of her neck in his palm. His lips plucked tenderly, lovingly, at hers. She tasted so good. He wondered if he'd ever tire of the sweet flavor of her lips. Her skin. As his body stirred, Donovan wondered how he could be wanting her so soon again.

"All those cold, lonely showers did wonders for my gas bill."

"Speaking of showers . . ." As Brooke trailed her fingernail down his thigh, she heard his quick intake of breath.

In an instant, Donovan was on his feet with Brooke in his arms as he strode purposefully toward her bathroom. "I've just discovered the perfect argument for making love here more often. Instead of my place."

She lifted a brow. "Considering your initial complaints, Donovan, I can't wait to hear the explanation for your sudden change in heart."

He pressed a quick hard kiss against her lips. "I can't think of anything I'd rather do than spend the rest of my life taking long, luxurious showers with my sexy wife. And let's face it, sweetheart, with your portfolio of trust funds, you can afford a lot more hot water than the pittance this college pays me will buy."

Brooke's hair trailed over his arm as she tilted her head back and laughed appreciatively. "Professor Kincaid," she drawled, her lips curved in a warm, feminine smile, "I do like your style."

"What are you going to tell the board of regents?" Donovan asked later that afternoon.

In the process of taking two packages of homemade fettuccine from the freezer, Brooke looked back over her shoulder curiously. "About what?"

As he uncorked the bottle of California chardonnay, Donovan knew Alex would approve of Brooke's taste. Even the label looked expensive. "About us."

She shrugged as she crossed the kitchen to the microwave. "I hadn't planned to tell them anything. I certainly don't have a clause in my contract that prohibits me from marrying." She smiled her thanks as Donovan handed her a glass of wine.

He gave her a long, considering look. "I'll have to admit to worrying that once we'd made love, you'd postpone the wedding."

Brooke had been about to take a sip of the chilled white wine. At his words, she placed her glass deliberately on the counter. Going up on her toes, she linked her fingers around his neck, drawing his head down.

"Why on earth would I do that?" she asked, brushing her lips against his. Brooke couldn't recall ever feeling as happy, as fulfilled, as she did at this moment. "Just because you turned me down once, Donovan Kincaid, don't think I'm going to let you get away again."

"So who's trying to get away?" He deepened the kiss.

Engulfed in a renewed tide of desire, Brooke was stunned by the urgency of her need for Donovan again so soon after having made love. Would she never get enough of him, she wondered through her whirling senses.

It took a moment for the sound of breaking glass to register. When it did, they both looked down at what remained of Donovan's wineglass.

"I suppose that was Waterford," he offered after a lengthy pause.

"Don't worry about it." Brooke brushed off his concern airily. "Actually, if you want to know the truth, I was getting rather tired of the pattern. After all, that set of crystal has been in my family since before I was born."

Donovan groaned. "If you're trying to make me feel better about breaking a family heirloom, Brooke, you're not doing a very good job."

She nodded gravely. "I see what you mean. I suppose, being a man of honor, that you'll want to pay off your debt."

"Of course," he agreed immediately.

Donovan wondered if she'd be willing to accept time payments. How much did that stuff cost, anyway? His own collection of wineglasses and beer mugs came embossed with the name of a local pizza chain.

Brooke chewed thoughtfully on a rose-tinted fingernail. "I suppose I could take a personal check," she said slowly. "Of course, there may just be another way to handle the problem."

"Another way?" There was no mistaking the teasing gold lights in her tawny eyes.

"You could always work it off."

"I used to mow lawns when I was a kid," he offered helpfully.

Her lips were drawn into a slight frown, but the laughter still danced in her eyes. "I live in an apartment, Donovan, remember? I don't have a lawn."

"Sounds as if we have a problem."

"There must be some small task you could perform." Her voice was soft, breathless. "You must have some talent. Something you do better than anyone else."

Donovan feigned shock. "Why, Ms Stirling, are you suggesting that I sell my body in order to pay off a wineglass?"

"Not merely any old wineglass. It *was* Waterford," she reminded him sternly.

"Well, hell, that makes all the difference." Their eyes held, sharing the laughter, before Donovan lowered his head and kissed her soundly. "How's that for a down payment?"

Brooke skimmed a finger down his jawline. "I think you'll do just fine, Professor Kincaid."

"Just fine?" he challenged softly, tangling his hands in her hair as he tilted her head back.

Brooke closed her eyes to the flare of heat as Donovan kissed her with a pent-up hunger that was stunning in its intensity.

"You're right," she said breathlessly. "You're much, much better than fine. A superior, at the very least."

"Hot damn," Donovan said happily as he released her, locating a broom in a nearby closet, "wait until Serena and Alex hear that I'm moonlighting as a love slave."

"Only until you get the wineglass paid off," Brooke reminded him.

He was plucking the larger shards of glass from the puddle of spilled white wine. "How long do you think that will be?"

Brooke's smile blossomed on her face. "Oh, fifty or sixty years, at the very least."

Donovan's bright green eyes returned her smile. "Lady, you've got yourself a deal."

During the light supper, Donovan recalled the question that had been nagging at the back of his mind all afternoon.

"You really don't expect any problem with the board?" he asked, breaking off a piece of crusty French bread from the loaf in the center of the table.

Immersed in the lingering joy of their lovemaking, Brooke had entirely forgotten about their earlier conversation. She didn't want to talk about her work. She didn't want to think about it. Not today. Not this perfect, love-filled day.

"Honestly, Donovan," she protested mildly, "I can't imagine why you believe the board of regents could care one way or the other whom I marry."

"Under normal circumstances, they probably wouldn't," he agreed. "But aren't we inviting conjecture when you announce our marriage plans right after approving my funding?"

Brooke's blood ran cold. Her fingers trembled visibly as she lowered her fork to the table. "You know I can't talk about that," she protested in a tone she wished had been stronger.

"I know," he agreed patiently, spreading a light herb-flavored butter onto his bread. "But after today we certainly don't have any secrets from each other."

When she didn't answer, he looked up at her curiously. "We don't, do we, Brooke?"

Her words blocked by the enormous lump in her throat, Brooke could only shake her head. Donovan would've had to have been blind to miss the stricken look on her face.

"Brooke," he repeated slowly, carefully, "there isn't anything you want to tell me, is there?"

Her soft sigh was audible in the suddenly still air. "Oh, Donovan—"

Anger. It flared, illogically, inexplicably. Donovan didn't know which made him more furious. The idea that Brooke was obviously prepared to reject his proposal, knowing how vital the funds were to his work. Or the fact that she had kept her intentions from him, making love with him as if she cared. As if she loved him as deeply, as irrevocably, as he loved her.

"I see." He bit the words off through clenched teeth as he rose from the table.

The dangerous fire in his eyes was intimidating. "No, you don't," she said, reaching out a hand. "Please, sit down and I'll explain everything."

Donovan was unaware of his fingers clenching and unclenching into fists. All he knew was that he was furious. And that he felt like hell.

"Just tell me one thing."

Did that icy, unfeeling voice belong to the same man who'd murmured words of love, of passion, in her ears only an hour ago? How could that possibly be? As she forced herself to meet his grim gaze, Brooke saw her blissful future slipping away like grains of sand through her fingertips.

"Anything."

"My proposal. Did you approve it? All of it?"

She dragged her hand through her hair, desperately seeking the words that would help him understand. "Not exactly."

"Not exactly," he repeated roughly. "What the hell does that mean? Either you did approve the funds. Or you didn't. You can't have it both ways."

She was on her feet, moving around the table to grab his arms. "I approved the important parts."

"It's all important, Brooke. At least it is to me."

At his cold, implacable tone, the first hint of anger shot into Brooke's eyes. She dropped her hands to her side. "Damn it, haven't you ever heard of compromise?" she demanded furiously.

"Not where my work is concerned." Donovan's tone was calm. Final.

Brooke swallowed, fighting back tears. "So where does that leave us?"

From his dispassionate stare, Brooke had no way of knowing that Donovan felt as if his heart was being torn to shreds. He recalled a time, not so very long ago, when he had felt almost smug, watching Alex and Serena struggle through the trials and tribulations of their love affair. He had decided then that since love seemed to turn intelligent people into blithering idiots, he'd just as soon pass on the entire experience. It was coming as an unpleasant surprise to discover that he hadn't had any choice in the matter from the beginning.

"That's up to you, Brooke," he answered at length.

There was a tug-of-war going on inside of her. Part of Brooke longed to approve Gloria's damned television, her intended mate, all of Donovan's proposal. Another more rational self pointed out that such action would only be delaying the inevitable. With the exception of reversing her cuts to General Osborne, the board had seconded her decision on every single issue. She could stamp *approved* all over Donovan's inviolate proposal and the board would still reject those items they viewed as superfluous.

"I can't change things, Donovan," she said truthfully, regretfully.

He shoved his hands into his pockets to keep from hitting the wall. "Well, that's that. Looks like I'd better get Gloria fitted for snowshoes." He turned, heading toward the door.

Brooke remained rooted to the spot. "What does that mean?" A nagging little suspicion teased at the back of her mind, but she couldn't believe it. "You're not leaving Claremont?"

He paused in the doorway, flashing her a grim, mirthless smile. "I've always admired your ability to read between the lines, Brooke. When you make your report public tomorrow, you can also inform the board that I'll be spending next year in Ithaca."

She felt her heart sink to the gray tile floor. "Cornell offered you a position." It was not a question.

"As well as agreeing to my proposal. Each and every item," he tacked on significantly.

"But your work here, with the other apes—"

"Will be carried on by someone else." He nodded. "Goodbye, Brooke. And good luck. Something tells me that after tomorrow you're going to need it."

With that he was gone. In an uncharacteristic display of temper, Brooke flung her wineglass after him. It hit the doorframe, shattering to the floor.

Then, cursing him and loving him at the same time, she broke down and cried.

It was nothing less than bedlam. Insanity reigned supreme in the hours following the board of regents' meeting. Brooke's phone had not stopped ringing since the announcement. All five buttons flashed with ominous orange lights, and if she had wanted to escape the constant stream of complainants, she would have been forced to climb out the window. Her outer office was jammed to the rafters with disgruntled faculty members, all waiting to lodge a formal complaint.

There were only two not represented. General Osborne certainly had no reason to argue the findings of the board. Unwilling to lose the political and financial clout the general brought to the college, the members of the board had unanimously approved his work in its entirety. The second member of the faculty who had failed to make an appearance was Donovan. But, Brooke thought grimly, eyeing the blinking lights, he had already let her know what he thought of her decision. In spades.

Closing her eyes on a weary sigh, Brooke buzzed Mrs. Harrigan. "Send in the next one," she said, her voice decidedly lacking in enthusiasm.

"At least you can't say that you're not in demand," a friendly feminine voice offered.

Brooke's eyes flew open to view Serena Bedare standing just inside the door. "If you're here about your husband's trip to the Middle East..."

"Alex and I have one rule," Serena said mildly, claiming a chair on the visitor's side of the desk in a fluid, graceful motion. "We never interfere with each other's work. Personally, I would have preferred he had gotten the funding. It would have given him the impetus he needed to return to his home for a visit." Her eyes shadowed momentarily with emotion. "He hasn't been back to Egypt since he buried his father."

As quick as the sorrow had appeared, it was gone. Serena's clear gray eyes met Brooke's. "Whatever my personal feelings, I wouldn't think to come begging favors for Alex. On the other hand, I can't sit idly by and watch you and Donovan throw away something worth fighting for."

Brooke began nervously gathering up the sheets of paper scattered over the top of her desk. "Did Donovan send you?"

A ghost of a smile hovered around the corners of Serena's lips. "What do you think?"

"I think he'd hit the roof if he knew you were interfering in his life."

"He said you were intelligent," Serena said as she allowed the smile to break free for a fleeting moment. "As for interfering, it's a sister's responsibility to speak up when she sees her brother making an ass of himself."

The smile disappeared as Serena's expression turned grave. She leaned forward in her chair. "He loves you, Brooke."

Unwilling to meet what she knew would be a sympathetic but argumentative gaze, Brooke kept her attention directed toward the stack of papers, lining up the ruffled edges with all the precision of a NATO general preparing for rifle inspection.

"He loves his work more."

Serena's blond hair whipped across her shoulders as she shook her head decisively. "No. He loves his work, yes. He could never have stuck with it for all these years if he didn't. Oh, I'll admit that Donovan can be infuriatingly dogmatic when it comes to his project, but it isn't a case of loving his research more than you. Or you more than his research. The two have nothing to do with each other."

"Perhaps they do," Brooke argued quietly. "More than you think."

Serena pursed her lips in thought. "I don't understand."

Brooke rose and went over to stare out the window. As if sensing the other woman's need to gather her thoughts, Serena remained silent.

"What if he only pretended to care for me? In order to ensure funding for his project." For the first time since Donovan had marched out of her apartment, she had spoken her secret fears out loud.

Serena's slight gasp was easily audible in the sudden stillness of the room. "You can't believe he'd be capable of such deceit!"

Brooke closed her eyes briefly. "I don't know what to believe."

"As devoted as my brother is to those damn apes, he could have accepted the loss of his funding."

"I doubt that," Brooke argued as she turned to face Serena. "Especially since he seems quite prepared to run off to Cornell. Again."

"Did you ever think that he isn't running *to* Cornell?" Serena asked quietly. "That he's running *away* from here? From you?"

"That's ridiculous." Exasperated, confused, unhappy, Brooke refused to consider the notion.

Serena's frustrated sigh ruffled her bangs. "For two supposedly intelligent individuals, you and my brother take the cake for muleheaded stupidity."

She shook her head, her eyes laced with a very real regret. "For your information, Brooke, Donovan rejected Cornell's offer the week you arrived on campus. He never had any intention of moving his project to New York. Not until yesterday."

With that closing statement Serena left the office. Brooke was debating following her when the irritating buzz of the intercom signaled yet another complainant.

A week passed without any word from Donovan. Seven very long, very lonely days. Brooke learned, through the grapevine, that he was out of town. She could only assume he was in Ithaca, making arrangements for his move. The rebellion among the faculty members had settled down to a dull roar, and despite the decidedly uncomplimentary cartoons appearing in the student newspaper—one depicting Brooke as the Queen of Hearts ordering the decapitation of a blond-tressed Gloria clad in Alice in Wonderland's white pinafore— people begrudgingly began to accept the fact that the money tree had temporarily dried up.

Meanwhile, given sufficient time to consider her feelings for Donovan in depth, Brooke made the decision that he was not going to get away with simply cutting and running. Not this time. Although she regretted the college losing him, Brooke was prepared to accept Donovan's need to continue his work in more economically favorable conditions. But if he thought that he could walk away from her without so much as a backward glance, he had another think coming.

Monday afternoon Brooke tidied up her desk, preparing to leave her office early. On her way out, she stopped by Mrs. Harrigan's desk.

"If anyone is looking for me," she informed her secretary, "I'll be unavailable until tomorrow morning."

The woman nodded an iron-gray head. "After last week's three-ring circus, you could certainly use a little time off," she agreed. "Good luck."

"Good luck?"

Steady, knowing eyes met Brooke's curious gaze through thick lenses. "You are going over to straighten things out with Professor Kincaid, aren't you?"

Of course she was, Brooke acknowledged inwardly. While she had no idea what she was going to do, or say, she had no intention of leaving Donovan's house until she had bridged the gulf between them. Brooke had made that decision days ago. But she certainly hadn't breathed a word of her plans to anyone. Not even Serena, who had called her daily with encouraging words.

"What makes you think I'm seeing Donovan?"

Mrs. Harrigan shrugged. "Since his plane got in fifteen minutes ago, and it's a ten-minute drive from the Ontario airport, it doesn't exactly take a Rhodes scholar to figure out where you're headed."

Her expression softened, appearing almost motherly in its concern. "He's such a nice young man, dear. Oh, his lack of punctuality leaves a great deal to be desired, and you should probably inspect his clothing before he leaves the house each morning, but I can certainly think of worse character flaws in a man, can't you?"

Brooke's gaze slid through the doorway to her desk where the blue paperweight caught the early afternoon light. For a man totally deficient in decorating skills, the fact that Donovan had chosen the ideal gift displayed the amount of time and effort involved in its purchase. He wouldn't have gone to so much trouble unless he honestly loved her.

"I certainly can," Brooke agreed softly.

"Of course you can," Mrs. Harrigan returned assuredly. Her smile widened. "Don't let him get away."

Brooke laughed as she headed toward the door. "I don't intend to," she said with renewed conviction.

Donovan saw her the moment he turned the corner. She was sitting on the porch swing, looking as beautiful, as composed, as ever. Only the swinging of her foot revealed that she was as uncomfortable with this situation as he was.

All week he had picked up the phone to call her, wanting to set things right between them. But each time he'd lowered the receiver to its cradle, deciding that what he needed to say would be better said in person. Only Serena's continual assurance that she was keeping in touch with Brooke had kept him from returning before concluding his meetings.

He slipped his hand into his pocket, his fingers curling around the worn Lincoln penny. He'd found it while packing. Searching under the bed for a pair of matching socks, Donovan had come across the forgotten talisman. Feeling admittedly foolish, he had not been able to resist its silent appeal. During the long week away from Brooke, he had found the coin brought a strangely calming confidence. Not that he was at all superstitious, Donovan assured himself, as he had been doing over and over again these past seven days. The penny merely represented his sister's support. And love.

At the familiar sound of the MG's engine, Brooke lifted her head, her breath stopping in her throat as she waited for Donovan to pull the sports car into the driveway. She wiped her hands surreptitiously on her russet skirt, wondering at the ability of an ice-cold hand to perspire. *Oh God,* she thought frantically, *how do I begin?*

As he exited the car, Donovan's carefully rehearsed speech fled from his mind. All the words of regret, contrition, love, disappeared as if expunged from a slate. All he could do was stand at the bottom of the porch steps and stare up at her.

Her sleek chestnut hair skimmed her shoulders in a smooth, straight line. Her classically tailored linen suit was dark, her blouse a shade of burnished gold that enhanced her eyes. Brooke's only jewelry was a pair of gold stud earrings and her watch. A pair of nutmeg pumps completed a look that Donovan knew was designed to make her appear coolly competent. Professional.

However, on closer study, her bottom lip, caught unconsciously in her teeth, gave away her discomfort with their situation. Experiencing a wild surge of hope, Donovan unconsciously rubbed the lucky talisman.

"Brooke."

He managed a polite nod when what he really longed to do was sweep her into his arms, carry her into the house and spend the rest of the afternoon and all of the night making love to her.

He certainly wasn't going to make it easy on her, Brooke acknowledged with an inner sigh. "Hello, Donovan," she said quietly. "Welcome home. How were things in Ithaca?"

He opened his mouth to explain his sudden disappearance when the phone began to ring. "Damn," he muttered, dropping his suitcase to begin searching under the clay pots for his spare key. He'd misplaced the one he usually carried on his key ring somewhere in London last summer and had put off getting a replacement.

"Here." Brooke handed him the brass key. "It's always under the third pot from the left."

"Wish I could remember that," he muttered, unlocking the oak door as the telephone continued its insistent demand.

"Perhaps you need someone to take care of all those irritating little details," Brooke suggested with undue casualness.

Donovan stopped abruptly in the act of opening the door to give Brooke his full attention. Something flashed in his eyes. Something subtle. Indiscernible.

"Perhaps I do," he said after a lengthy pause.

As their eyes met and held, Brooke couldn't have moved if she had wanted to. "Your phone's still ringing."

That fierce, dangerous fire that she had seen only once before flared in his eyes. "Damn the phone." He moved toward her, reaching out to grasp her wrist. Brooke's pulse speeded up under his fingertips. "We have to talk."

"Yes." She wondered if Donovan realized that she was agreeing to much more than conversation.

Her eyes—those gorgeous, sensual eyes that had kept him awake most of this past week—darkened in response to his thumb brushing against her skin. Donovan reminded himself that nothing would be settled by taking Brooke to bed before they had discussed their future. But oh, how he ached for her. The telephone had not ceased ringing; its shrill demand infiltrated the frozen moment, shattering the silken mood.

He shook his head in mute frustration. "Brooke—"

"Whoever it is isn't going to go away," she said reluctantly.

As Donovan entered the house, he decided he could quite cheerfully wring the neck of whoever was on the other end of the phone.

"What is it?" he answered harshly. "Look, Stephanie, I just got in. Let me call you later, okay?"

Brooke had followed Donovan into the house. As she watched, his green eyes darkened to a stormy sea. "What?" he exploded. "I'll be right there." His knuckles, as he hung up the telephone, were white.

Ice rippled down Brooke's spine. She reached out, placing her hand on Donovan's arm. "What is it?"

"It's Gloria."

Her stomach twisted at the raw pain in Donovan's voice. "Oh no. Is she ill?"

He dragged his hands through his dark hair. "Worse."

"Not—" Brooke couldn't say the word.

"She's gone."

"Gone? Are you saying someone kidnapped her?"

His gaze was as distant as she had ever seen it. "She's run away." He shook off her light touch. "I've got to find her. Before the police do. There's no telling what they'll do to her."

Brooke had a very good idea of what the authorities would do to Gloria. And it wasn't at all pleasant. "I'm coming with you," she insisted, following him out of the house.

"That isn't necessary."

She was in the passenger seat of the MG before he could turn the key. "Gloria knows me. Besides, you're going to need all the help you can get."

"That's a fact," he muttered, pulling out of the driveway, headed toward the compound. "Damn!" He slammed the heel of his hand on the top of the steering wheel. "If only I'd been here."

"Do you have any idea why she left?" Brooke asked, holding onto the edge of her seat as the MG tore around a curve.

"Yeah." He slanted her a grim look. "Her television blew up last night. Stephanie tried to tell her that I'd be home today, but I guess she didn't trust me any longer."

Brooke felt the knot in her stomach tighten. "Donovan, about your funding—"

He shook his head as he pulled the car up in front of the center with a shuddering halt. "No," he insisted harshly. "Not now."

"But—"

He cut her off, slicing the air with a furious hand. "This isn't any time to discuss it, Brooke." He was out of the car, headed toward the office on a run. Unable to do anything else, Brooke swallowed her apology and followed him.

Chapter Thirteen

It had grown dark. A full moon hovered overhead, cold and watchful in a sky strangely empty of stars. Spotlights cast long, yellow shadows over the landscape and the lonely baying of dogs filled the night air as the searchers made their way in teams back and forth across the San Bernardino Mountains just north of the campus.

"We'll find her," Brooke kept insisting as she and Donovan made their way up the hillside where Gloria had last been seen. The family of picnickers had been understandably startled by the sudden appearance of a *Gorilla gorilla beringei* in their midst.

Donovan's bleak gaze moved to the armed men who were methodically sweeping the area in long lines. "But will we find her before they do? That's the question."

"Of course we will," Brooke answered, wishing she could fully believe her emphatically issued statement.

The dogs, the men, the searchlights, all had to have Gloria frightened out of her wits. The chances of her coming out of hiding of her own free will were slim to nonexistent.

As they crisscrossed the mountainside, they came across Alex and Serena, who, along with several other students and faculty members, had joined the search for the runaway gorilla.

"I know it's just a matter of time," Serena assured her brother.

"She's always been a stubborn old girl," Alex added. "Perhaps I should have brought along my ukulele."

"We want to coax her out of hiding, darling," Serena said. "Not give her a reason to run farther."

"She liked my singing well enough when I distracted her so Donovan and I could watch you on the news that night," Alex reminded his wife amiably.

"That's it!" Brooke exclaimed.

Three pairs of curious eyes turned toward her. "What's it?" Donovan asked without a great deal of enthusiasm.

"Donovan, let me have the keys to the van." Brooke held out her hand.

"Why?"

"I'll explain when I get back."

"The van is college property, Brooke. I don't think you're authorized to drive it."

Brooke knew it was a sign of how upset Donovan was that he'd even bring that little matter up. In all the years she'd known him, Brooke had yet to see him pay any attention to rules or regulations, unless they were written in his favor.

"You need to stay here in case they find Gloria," she pointed out. "Besides, we don't have time to argue," she insisted. "Just let me borrow the van for ten or fifteen minutes and I think I can solve our problem."

Donovan shrugged, reaching into his pocket. As his fingers brushed the lucky penny, they squeezed instinctively, wishfully. The others waited with barely restrained impatience as he continued searching, finally locating the vehicle key in an inside jacket pocket.

"I'll be right back," Brooke said, going up on her toes to brush a quick, reassuring kiss against his cheek. Before he could answer, she was running back to where they'd left the van at a mountain viewpoint turnoff.

"Well," Serena said as they watched Brooke tear back down the curving road, "at least your life together isn't going to be dull, brother, dear."

Donovan rubbed his cheek where he could still feel the warmth of Brooke's lips. "I suppose it won't," he agreed flatly. Then, shaking his head, he looked back toward the searchers making their way nearer and nearer the summit of Mount Baldy. "I suppose we'd better get back to work."

As he walked away, Serena and Alex exchanged a helpless look before rejoining the search.

Brooke's errand took no more than fifteen minutes, but it had seemed a lifetime as she had driven at a speed that would have earned her a hefty ticket, had any troopers stopped her. Fortunately the majority of law enforcement officers were on the mountain, searching for Gloria.

"Do you know where you're going?" Donovan asked as she tore around the curves. She had stopped just long enough to pick him up before continuing her quest.

"Of course." Brooke had to force her eyes to remain open as she swerved to miss an oncoming four-wheel-drive truck. "Damn. I thought they cleared everyone off the mountain."

"Those two must have been off the beaten track. Remember how we used to love to find little out-of-the-way places to neck?" As soon as he'd said the words, Donovan heard a bell chime in the far reaches of his mind. "The cave," he said suddenly.

Brooke flashed him a quick, congratulatory grin. "We've all combed every inch of this mountain without finding her. So unless Gloria's sprouted wings and flown away, she'll be there. It's the only place left."

Donovan returned Brooke's smile as he ruffled her hair. "That is brilliant deductive reasoning, love."

Love. Was there a more wonderful word in the dictionary? As she risked taking her eyes from the roadway again, Brooke's expression turned serious. "I do love you, Donovan," she said suddenly.

His smile moved to his eyes, dazzling in its warmth. "I know. And I love you. But—" he cringed as the right wheels of the van slid onto the shoulder of the road, scattering gravel "—do you think we could discuss this later?"

"Coward," she retorted, twisting the steering wheel to return the vehicle to the asphalt roadway.

"I just want us to return from this adventure in one piece, Brooke. Spending my honeymoon in a body cast isn't my idea of fun."

"Speaking of fun," Brooke said as she came to a stop with a squeal of brakes, "are you going to make love with me once we get Gloria tucked in again, all safe and sound?"

"What do you think?

Donovan ignored the smell of burning rubber as he leaned over to kiss Brooke for the first time since he had arrived home more than three hours ago. Her lips parted and as she responded with a ferocity that fully equaled his own, Donovan nearly forgot his reason for being on the mountain.

"Wow," Brooke said, reluctantly tilting her head back to break the heated contact. "If that's the way you kiss when you return from New York, I suppose I shouldn't complain about you going to Cornell."

Her face was flushed with emotion, her eyes gleaming in the stark moonlight with unmistakable pleasure. Donovan couldn't imagine anyone appearing more lovely than Brooke did at this moment.

"I'm not going to Cornell."

Her eyes widened. "But I thought—"

Donovan knew that if he tried to explain things now, it would only waste precious time. "Later," he suggested with a coaxing smile.

It only took Brooke a moment to decide her priorities. She and Donovan had a lifetime to settle their misunderstandings. The important thing was to locate Gloria before some tragic incident occurred.

"Later," she agreed. "And it better be good."

From her warning tone, Donovan knew that Brooke wasn't going to give in all that easily. While he had no doubt that she'd agree to marry him, his intuition told him that she had every intention of making him work for it.

Brooke reached behind her to retrieve her portable battery-operated television from the back seat. "Bait," she answered Donovan's questioning look.

His expression was filled with heartfelt admiration. "Not bad, lady. Not bad at all."

As they made their way to the secret cavern in the side of the mountain that they had discovered so many years ago, he slipped his hand into his pocket, receiving a certain inexplicable comfort from Serena's coin.

"I don't remember this place being so spooky," Brooke whispered as they entered the black, silent cave. Her voice echoed off the stone walls. "Remind me never to come here again at night."

"It's just as dark in the daytime, Brooke," Donovan pointed out with maddening accuracy. "Once you get past the first turn."

"Since you insist on maintaining your reputation as a rational scientist type, Professor Kincaid, you, of all people should know that bats sleep in the daytime."

His laughter reverberated around them. "There aren't any bats in here."

"Are you sure?"

"Positive."

"Well," she countered, sounding unconvinced, "I sure hope you know your bats as well as you do your gorillas, Donovan." She peered into the black void beyond the scant illumination offered by the yellow beam of his flashlight. "How much farther do you think we need to go?"

Donovan glanced back over his shoulder. The entry to the cave had been swallowed up by the darkness. "This should be far enough," he decided.

"That's precisely what I wanted to hear," Brooke said with a deep sigh of relief. "I don't think we're going to get a very good picture in here," she complained, fiddling with the antenna of the television. "The cave walls are blocking the signal."

"All we need is to get her attention."

"I hate it when you turn logical on me." She continued twisting the dial until she located a syndicated program of *Kojak*. "Now, hopefully all we have to do is wait." She took a seat on a flat rock, prepared to watch Telly Savalas solve the crime.

Donovan sat down beside her. "Want to make out while we wait for Gloria to make her appearance?" he asked, putting his arm around her.

Brooke experienced a thrill of pleasure as his lips brushed her temple. "Don't tempt me," she complained. "You've no idea how miserable I've been all week, Donovan Kincaid."

He nibbled at her earlobe. "Not as miserable as I've been."

"Want to bet?"

He placed a light kiss against the top of her head. "We'll argue it out when we get back home. How are you at wrestling?"

She smiled. "Two out of three pins?"

Donovan chuckled, drawing her into his arms. "At least."

They sat there, arms entwined, for the next forty-five minutes. *Kojak* gave way to *Gunsmoke*, which while not technically a police show, hopefully had enough gunfire to draw Gloria's interest. Meanwhile, outside the cave, they could hear the howls of the dogs and the shouts of the men as they drew nearer.

"This isn't going to work, after all," Brooke said on a sad little sigh as the credits rolled on the screen.

Donovan hugged her tighter. "It was a great idea, sweetheart."

"If it was such a hot idea, it would have worked," she pointed out, tears of frustration brightening her eyes. "Damn it, this is all my fault."

Donovan was stunned by how harshly Brooke's tears affected him. As long as he had known her, as intimate as they had been, he had never seen Brooke Stirling cry. When she gave in to her grief, wrapping her arms around him to bury her face against his shoulder, Donovan attempted to soothe her. His fingers combed unsteadily through her hair, his hands made calming, ineffective circles against her back. Suddenly he froze.

"Brooke," he whispered, "don't move."

She immediately went rigid in his arms. "Is it—"

"It sure as hell is." His soft voice was triumphant. They held their breaths, waiting for the gorilla to make the first move.

The small black and white television gave off a soft glow that illuminated the immediate surrounding area. Gloria slowly, tentatively, entered the circle of muted light, her black eyes flashing as they raked over Donovan and Brooke.

"Gloria hungry," she signed imperiously.

"Come home with us and we'll feed you right away," Donovan agreed expansively. "Anything you want."

The dark eyes cut to the television. "Want television," she insisted firmly.

"You've got it," Donovan assured her. "It'll be delivered tomorrow morning."

The gorilla's broad dark face revealed her skepticism. "New television? Really?"

"With a larger screen than your old one," he coaxed.

She seemed to be considering this. "Gloria come home."

Donovan nodded formally. "I'm glad."

"Want peanut butter," she insisted as the three of them left the cave. "And Jell-O. And banana milk shake."

Donovan laughed as he opened the back door of the van. "You can have anything your little gorilla heart desires."

They stopped just long enough to assure the searchers that everything was well in hand. The men were openly relieved not to be faced with the task of trapping a two-hundred-plus pound gorilla. The dogs, however, did not appear eager to return to the trucks. At the moment Gloria was content, watching Brooke's portable TV in the back seat of the van.

"What are you going to do when she discovers you lied about the television?" Brooke said under her breath as they drove back down the mountain.

"Me? Lie to a gorilla? How can you accuse your fiancé of such a terrible act?" Donovan shook his head with mock regret. "I'm disappointed in you, Brooke."

Brooke was confused. "But you told me that you're not going to Cornell."

"I'm not," Donovan agreed. "Look at her," he said happily, casting a quick glance into the rearview mirror. "From the way she's behaving you'd never know how much trouble she caused today."

"Donovan," Brooke said hesitantly, "I do honestly love you—"

"And you've no idea how happy that makes me," he broke in, giving her a warm, loving grin.

"But I still can't give you the television."

"Of course you can't, honey."

She couldn't understand his sudden cheerfulness. The last time they had discussed his funding, Donovan had been angry enough to chew nails.

"You accepted the money from Serena and Alex," she guessed.

"Nope."

"From Stavros?"

"I told you I wasn't about to take anything from him," Donovan reminded her. "He and Anna aren't getting any younger. They can't run that place forever."

"Then where—"

He flashed her a bold, rakish grin. "I worked out a deal with the computer company."

"What computer company?"

"The one I use for Gloria's language experiments," he said patiently. "They were more than willing to spring for the cost of a new television in exchange for Gloria's appearance in their new advertising campaign." He rubbed his jaw. "Do you have any idea how much money is involved in advertising? I was honestly amazed. Perhaps we've gotten into the wrong business."

Donovan's grin widened. "Anyway, they even threw in a VCR. Wait until Gloria finds out that she's going to be able to tape her favorite shows. She'll be in gorilla heaven."

Brooke hated bursting Donovan's little bubble of contentment by sounding like a bureaucrat, but she had to ask. "Shouldn't you have gotten the college's permission?"

He shrugged. "Why? Gloria's mine, Brooke. She doesn't belong to the college."

"Still, they might object to being featured in commercial advertising," she cautioned carefully.

Donovan gave her a slow, easy smile. "Do you think a contribution to the college coffers will soothe their objections?"

Her eyes narrowed. "How much?"

When he named an amount more than three times the total of this year's entire operating budget, Brooke assured herself that Donovan had to be joking.

Her stunned expression drew a deep laugh. "Not a bad week's work, was it?"

Brooke found his grin both attractive and infuriating. She swore as her temper flared. "Do you have any idea how much grief you could have saved me if you'd just gone to them in the beginning?''

"I didn't think of them in the beginning," he answered mildly. He reached out to trace a finger along her bottom lip. "I've missed the taste of this beautiful mouth."

Brooke tossed her head as she glared at him. "I suppose you think you can sweet-talk your way out of all this."

"I was hoping to give it the old college try," Donovan drawled as he pulled the van up in front of the gorilla compound. "Come on, kiddo," he said over his shoulder. "It's time to hit the hay. And not a moment too soon," he murmured to Brooke who glanced back at the gorilla. Gloria's huge head was bobbing sleepily.

"I'll be back as soon as I tuck her in," Donovan promised.

"And then we're going to settle this once and for all," Brooke insisted. "You've a lot to answer for, Donovan Kincaid. You let me think you were leaving town, you cost me a week's sleep, you—"

He cut her off with a hard demanding kiss that took her breath away. "I'll be right back."

Her head swirling, Brooke could only nod impotently, wishing that she could at least work up some genuine antagonism as Donovan flashed her a smug, self-satisfied smile. She leaned her head against the back of the seat and closed her eyes.

"Your place or mine?" Donovan asked when he returned.

"Classy line," she muttered, refusing to look at him. "Don't tell me you usually get results with such a tired old cliché?"

"You tell me." He bent down, skimming his lips up her cheeks, brushing against her temple, trailing down the bridge of her nose. "Is it working?"

As his tantalizing lips moved over her closed lids, Brooke felt as if he had taken a sparkler to her skin. She slowly opened her eyes.

"I don't know. Perhaps you ought to try it again."

"Good idea." His hands dove into her hair as his mouth fixed on hers in a series of slow kisses that had them both wanting more. Brooke's breathing grew ragged as her hands moved over his body, wanting, needing his strength. His love.

"How about we flip for it," he asked against her mouth.

Brooke caught the Lincoln penny in mid-toss. "Your place," she said. "It's closer."

"Alone at last." Donovan drew Brooke into his arms, burying his face against the side of her neck. "God, I thought we'd never get away. Coming down here to Melbourne for Serena's tournament was a dumb idea. We've barely had a minute to ourselves."

Brooke pressed her hands against his chest. "We're alone now."

Tilting her face, he kissed her tenderly. "You're a good sport, sweetheart. Most women would object to spending their honeymoon surrounded by in-laws."

"Hey," she retorted with a quick grin, "you just happen to be talking to someone who figured she'd be spending her honeymoon with a bunch of apes. Besides, people are going to be talking about today's match for years; watching Serena win her Grand Slam was just about the most thrilling experience of my life."

"How would you like to spend the rest of the evening topping it?" he asked, nipping at her bottom lip.

Brooke's eyes sparkled up at him. "Pretty sure of yourself, aren't you, Professor Kincaid?"

"Pretty sure of us," he corrected huskily, running his hands up and down her back.

"Only pretty sure?" Brooke arched a brow. "Is this the same individual who not so very long ago gave me a lecture on the scientific method?"

"You're right," Donovan agreed readily, scooping her into his arms. "Come on, sweetheart, we're wasting valuable time that we should be spending on additional experimentation."

Her laughter was free and breezy as she twined her arms around his neck. "Who'd ever suspect that logic could be so much fun?"

Donovan's answering chuckle was muffled against Brooke's smiling mouth as he carried her into the bedroom.

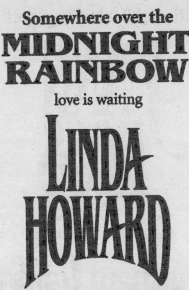

MIRA Books presents the newest
hardcover novel from

New York Times bestselling author

Experience the compelling story of

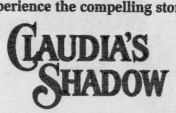

When her sister, Claudia, dies mysteriously,
Rowena Graham cannot accept the verdict of
suicide. Desperate to find out the truth, and to
discover why Claudia had been so difficult and
cruel, Rowena moves into Claudia's house—their
old family home. As she sorts out Claudia's affairs
Rowena discovers a trove of dark family secrets. And
finally sets herself free from the shadows of the past.

Look for *Claudia's Shadow* this May, wherever
hardcover books are sold.

MIRA **The brightest star in women's fiction**

Let this bestselling author introduce you to a sizzling new page-turner!

She'll do anything.

Lie, cheat, steal—Caroline Hogarth will do anything to get her little boy back. Her father-in-law will do anything to prevent it. And there's no one in the city he can't buy. Except, maybe, Jack Fletcher—a man Caroline is prepared to seduce.

So what if he's a convicted murderer? So what if he's a priest?

Watch the sparks fly this May.
Available wherever books are sold.

If you love the suspenseful tales of

JoANN ROSS

Order now for more thrilling stories
by one of MIRA's bestselling authors:

#66018	LEGACY OF LIES	$4.99 U.S.	☐
		$5.50 CAN.	☐
#66022	DUSK FIRE	$4.99 U.S.	☐
		$5.50 CAN.	☐
#66072	STORMY COURTSHIP	$4.99 U.S.	☐
		$5.50 CAN.	☐
#66092	CONFESSIONS	$4.99 U.S.	☐
		$5.50 CAN.	☐

(limited quantities available)

TOTAL AMOUNT	$
POSTAGE & HANDLING	$
($1.00 for one book, 50¢ for each additional)	
APPLICABLE TAXES*	$_____
TOTAL PAYABLE	$_____
(check or money order—please do not send cash)	

To order, send the completed form, along with a check or money order for
the total above, payable to MIRA Books, to: **In the U.S.:** 3010 Walden
Avenue, P.O. Box 9077, Buffalo, NY 14269-9077; **In Canada:** P.O. Box
636, Fort Erie, Ontario, L2A 5X3.

Name: _____

Address: _____ City: _____

State/Prov.: _____ Zip/Postal Code: _____

*New York residents remit applicable sales taxes.
Canadian residents remit applicable GST and provincial taxes.   MJRBL4

MIRA

Look us up on-line at: http://www.romance.net